Jimmy Jazz **III** Complete Works

1 House of the Unwed Mother

2 The Cadillac Tramps

3 The Sub

4 M-Theory

5 Rube Goldberg Suicide Machine

6 Where Life is Inappropriate

7 Home Despot

8 Nothing a Fire Can't Fix

9 This Ragged Muscle

10 The Book of Books

# RUBE GOLDBERG SUICIDE MACHINE

## A NOVEL BY JIMMY JAZZ

First Edition

ISBN:  978-1-7358686-1-5

Book Design: Jimmy Jazz

Garamond 3, Avenir & Times New Roman were used in the design of this book.

A version of this story appeared in 2003 at Jazz Shack Ink.

An audiobook read by the author was engineered by Korrey Lueders.

Pirate Enclave Books

https://pirateenclave.square.site

# Rube Goldberg Suicide Machine ⊖ a Novel

Heard a word, suicide.

Bad Religion

One man devised a Rube Goldberg contraption to prevent erection during sleep.

William S. Burroughs

Rube Goldberg Machine: A complex machine for a simple task.

# ONE

Mort Zazuzay stands in the kitchen staring into space. Snapping awake, he spends thirteen heartbeats trying to remember why he'd even gone into the kitchen. His heart beats eight more times before he takes a thin knife out of a wooden butcher block on the counter. It has a black plastic handle. The knife is poorly made but sharp. He holds the knife to his wrist and thinks about making an incision from the base of his hand up to the elbow. His heart beats five more times. He puts the knife back in the block. Pulls another knife from the block. Same cheap handle. The imprint at the base of the blade reads, Taiwan. This one is a steak knife. The blade is wider, stronger. It would make a quick deep cut. He looks down at a blue bucket with a wooden mop handle rising out of it. He pictures his blood flowing into the bucket. The brilliant blue, the pyrrole red. It's almost overwhelming. The steak knife hovers above the skin. It feels like more than the thought of suicide. As close as he's come. Three heartbeats. The steak knife slips back into place. He draws the butcher knife from the block. A knife for a slasher film. The knife he chops red bell peppers and brown onions with. A knife to mince garlic. This one diced a tomato at lunch. A piece of the tomato lays in its juice on the cutting board. Mort holds the knife to his wrist. He catches a reflection of himself in the toaster, the blonde wig, slightly off-kilter, surprises him. He'd forgotten that he was wearing it. His heart beats so loud he thinks someone is knocking at the door. Squeezing his fist, he slams his eyes shut with equal intensity.

His mother or a photograph of his mother as a young woman imposes itself:

1965. A young woman teases a platinum blonde wig into a flip and exhausts a can of aerosol to lock it in place. She straightens her Nylons, buttons her still-warm pant suit, the iron is unplugged at rest on top of a towel on the floor. She's beginning her adult life like the ones who pass between furnished rooms somewhere among the usual mixture of squares and streets. Even with the bed folded into a couch this particular room feels claustrophobic. The "blonde" climbs through the gloomy mist into a Volkswagen, which is olive green and will take her to work where she earns a dollar-twenty an hour, the money being pastel spring green, enough to feed one person, to pay rent, buy clothes and travel, a little, on holiday. You too can see the world, if you do your own hair and take your meals at home. Ha ha, what is this? I see a sailor in her future. They'll meet at a picnic. He'll stay the night too tired or too late to make it back to the base. They will fumble into sex. Conception will occur. The embryo will be allowed to develop. Another clichéd chorus in the song of sperm meets egg.

> Graduate high school, take one step
>
> Job in a keypunch, take one step
>
> Sleep with the sailor on shore leave
>
> You got pregnant, one step back
>
> Catch the ship, at the dock, take two steps
>
> In with the in-laws, middle class

Nine months later, Mort would kick out of his mother's womb and alter the trajectory of her life. Decide who you want to be or someone will. Someone small but demanding. It was the dawn of a nuclear family in the nuclear age, with but seven minutes to midnight he was born.

Nineteen years later, Mort found himself dancing the same steps, married with an apartment and a dull job. They started to collect electric can openers and couch pillows and toothbrushes in complementary colors.

His wife watches television in the so-called "living" room. He can hear the characters talking, gets caught up in the plot—has always been susceptible to narrative. The hand that holds the butcher knife shakes. He still hasn't remembered why he came into the kitchen. The show is less funny than its laugh track. It reminds him of a *Sanford and Son* episode where Lamont assumed his dad was dying of cancer. A miscommunication bit. The old, "I thought you were... ha ha" routine. The death gag. Redd Foxx was cool, he knew Malcolm X. One of the characters on this show thinks the other has AIDS. Samo situ for the millennium.

Mort thinks about his own son asleep in the bedroom. Well, supposed to be asleep, but caught in the narrative like his dad. Eyes closed, floating in the story, nothing else exists or matters. Earlier that evening the son got in the middle of an argument. That he sided with Mom shouldn't discount the value of an eight-year-old's wisdom. His wife likes to say Mort doesn't listen, but he recalls a series of rebukes, each overwriting one that came before.

> "Dad, Mom's right. You should listen. I don't like living in this roach infested rat trap. You are too fat. You smell bad even after you get out of the shower. I want a brother. That would make mom happy. Even a sister. Your hair is embarrassing. You need to get a job so we can move to a house with a backyard. It's not safe…"

Why do they punctuate their needs with tears?

Mort wanted to cry with them. Angora cried when she was upset, like there was a switch hidden behind those hazel orbs. It seems weird to say someone is good at crying, like a skill. If Mort has a switch, he supposes it's burnt. Like the bulb he means to change in the hall. He'd never seen his son cry much—not like this. There usually had to be some great strike to the psyche—a skinned knee, a splinter, a bee sting, that time a nail pushed through the rubber sole of his shoe into the tender flesh of his foot or when the cat got lost. Poor kitty. This seemed different.

"Mom, it seems like the only way we can get Dad to listen is to cry. I don't want to cry any more Mommy."

"You know Cubby cries himself to sleep."

"First I heard about it."

"You're so stingy—"

"I share everything."

"Taa. You don't pay attention. You don't."

Cubby was afraid of the dark, for one thing. And the desperate men who picked through the trash cans at night. He could hear them. Shifting around. They seemed unpredictable. They dressed in the garbage they picked through. They ate rotten food. And shouted at demons. You don't have to be desperate or hungry to want to sleep in a warm bed. They might kill or worse.

When Angora was a kid, the monstrous child dark made spooky by spirits lurking in the back of closets etched away any courage she gathered at the top of a tree she'd climbed or mid-cartwheel or holding her breath underwater in the "chester pool." Her mom's bible stories breathed life into the shadows. Her mom told her that spirits walked the world in search of bodies. Any body was better than no body. A spirit could possess a live pig. Just take control. A spirit could enter through a dirty mouth, even down there, so keep it clean, like a good girl, keep it shut.

Mort cried himself to sleep, once, blanket pulled up to his chin, worried about aliens—invaders from the outer limits on a mission to collect human specimens. They would take him up to their ship, back to their planet. Mort was sure they would come. He saw their shadows on the walls outside the window.

*Invaders from Mars! The Body Snatchers! The Thing!*

A teacher in high school claimed the green-tentacled aliens and flying saucers on tv were metaphors for the communist menace. So, he'd absorbed the paranoia of the age without knowing about brinkmanship, the bomb, HUAC, McCarthy or whatever U.S.S.R. stood for. No one talked about the proxy war in Vietnam or Agent Orange or the Pentagon Papers. If it was on the news, he was too busy throwing rocks at green plastic army men.

*Genocide! Slavery! Holocaust! Hiroshima!*

It made sense to cry yourself to sleep.

These thoughts, buried like land mines, push the knife flush against the skin of his forearm. He imagined his father walking in on him and imagined the subtle shift in the old man's countenance as he realized the horror in what was going on.

"What kind of wuss leaves a beautiful family like yours behind?"

It would be an honest question. A fair question Mort would consider, would chase, by Socratic method, and without sophistry, to its root. He knew his dad was the kind of person who would take suicide personally, like he'd made a mistake, failed.

"You never acted like this before your mother and I divorced."

But Mort didn't think of divorce that way, lots of kids lived with single moms and saw the father on weekends. It was normal. Maybe he was lucky, some kids never saw their "deadbeat" dads. "Broken Home" was a label someone made up like "freezer burn," "false prophet" or "living dead." A label that encouraged people not to look deeply. He didn't blame his parents for his low moods. His grandma had low moods, so did his uncles. They couldn't be held accountable for whatever obscene combination of genes they tossed together. Even when his dad criticized his art or denigrated his music, he felt like everyone was free to an opinion.

"You call that art? Disgusting, insulting, revolting garbage produced by a sick mind. You call this abomination music? This punk rock junk is trash."

He wished the opinions were backed by reason rather than adjectives or tautologies, some rationale besides what the neighbors thought. Like most people around here he didn't delve below the surface, seemed to be stuck at the level of appearance.

"Rip off the facade Dad! Come on. The noisy guitars are a gate, the lyrics are a barking dog to keep people like you at bay. Are you afraid of it because it shows the world the way it is? Is it too real? It's just 50s rocknroll played super-fast that doesn't deny we dropped the bomb."

In the midst of these "tirades," Mort's brain would repeat "I am my art, I am my music…" He didn't expect his dad to like it. It was there to challenge a corrupted genera-tion's values. To spit on the grave of commonplace as-sumptions. It was a war dance. Mort prized that it couldn't be used to sell soap on tv.

"Why don't you put on some decent clothes? Why don't you stop hanging around with these punks? You're better than that, better than a punk…"

"I don't want to keep up with the Joneses, picket fences or football. I'm a decent person. I care about the environment. I don't scapegoat immigrants or hate fags or call people retarded. You work in a bomb factory. Ha ha. That's crazy. You hang around with murderers…"

His dad saw it differently. He saw food on the table, a mortgage paid month by month over 30 years. It was what you were supposed to do. His dad wondered what happened to the sharp boy who learned to play chess? He was proud of the boy who loved sports and killed hours calculating his favorite ballplayers' stats. His father held that boy up high.

But Mort wanted to toss "Pride" out wholesale with reactionary emotions like "Shame." Shame made people feel bad about natural things they couldn't control like their body shape or sexual desires. It did little to regulate greed and mendacity.

The French philosopher Gilles Deleuze, who threw himself out of a window, said philosophy was useful for "turning stupidity into something shameful," which sounds like what Mort's friend Jimenez called "Awareness." Then again, Mort would toss out "clever" to rid the world of ignorance and love to get rid of hate.

If the wife or the kid walks in before he digs the blade into his arm, he can say he's putting away the dishes. But can he convince himself? Can he stand up to the feelings that push him around? Sure. Why not? He hadn't succumbed to peer pressure since Davy Wallz convinced him to dump his girlfriend in seventh grade. When Davy took his former girlfriend to the movies a week later, Mort took a lesson about people. He didn't smoke pot with his friends or snort coke on grad night with the "popular" crowd. He'd never cheated on a test at school or bought anything advertised in a commercial. Why listen to the little part of his brain that dragged him to the edge right now?

A sheen of sweat gathers on his corrugated forehead under strands of mop-like brown hair. Straight white teeth buttress pout-twisted lips. The anxious grimace is grotesque. This moment of mental anguish trains a wrinkle, as a river trains a canyon, across his brow.

He had always done what he thought was best. He calculated statistics, did research, estimated probabilities. He tried to do the right thing. He never rushed and though he never made any great mistakes neither had he carried off any great victory.

This last thought, about the insipid tenure of his life, is broken by a familiar sound floating in from the living room. The butcher knife slides back into the wooden block. He remembered The Clash saving his life as a teenager. He remembered the first time the needle hit the vinyl and the "electrical shocker" of sound that jumped into the room. Of course, this was the song, the one the radio played to death, that would be used to sell soap. Language has to be flayed and flogged to a pulp, so it can slip into the brain unawares. He should've seen it coming.

Leaning on the door jamb, Mort sees a car racing around. He doesn't know the make or model and doesn't care. It's a commercial. Those fuckers sold it. Nothing is sacred because nothing should be. That's the lesson. Everything is permitted. Guitarists and bass players and drummers need money. He shakes his face trying to buck the silly blonde wig. It falls away like the troubled grimace.

"Honey, you're right. We need to live our lives differently. I know what a stubborn ass I can be. I've always been resistant to change. Tomorrow I'm going to look for a new job, so we can move from this dump and you and Cubby can have decent things. I've been selfish. Like you said, my paintings haven't sold and it doesn't look like they will. So, fuck it. I can put my "hobby" on hold, do for you guys."

His wife looks up at him from the couch. The urge to be elated swells. She wants to be supportive, excited, but she's heard this speech. Next, he'll suggest they have another baby. She's lived with Mort long enough to recognize his attention cry. Like a sprouted seed, he wants sun and water in the human forms of love and affection. He wants to be caressed like a leafy houseplant by carbon dioxide and she knows… deprivation will force change. He needs to adapt under harsh conditions. Even if it means mutation. At risk of extinction.

She has survived the famine of his "art career." She's gone without new clothes while her friends shopped on payday. She stays home while those friends go to movies and out to restaurants. She's eaten pasta with plastic packets of ketchup or rice with soy sauce and Mort's home cooked beans for a decade. The thought of another pinto bean repulses her.

She wants the change he promised. She smiles weakly. The picture on the tv rolls. She adjusts the antenna, the screen shows a woman doubled, like a near-death out-of-body experience. Her attention drifts back to the situation comedy on the television away from the situation comedy of her marriage.

Later that night, Mort climbs into bed with her. Usually, after a domestic squall, he sleeps on the couch. She wears sweat shorts and an X-Large T-shirt. He slips out of his jeans which fall to the ground. Three nickels and two pennies roll out of the pocket into a dark recess under the bed. He stands naked—underwear in the laundry. Angora hasn't squirreled away quarters enough to do the wash.

"You eat too much cheese," his friend Jimenez counseled. "Cheese consumption leads to skid marks on your

underwear. Eat vegetables and stink less. You won't have to
do laundry all the time. Perishables or perish, Homie. Do
it for the planet."

Mort pushes his body up against his wife. His foot touches
her foot under the covers. She lies face down in a half-fetal
position with one leg straight back. They attach like
spoons in a silverware drawer. He slips a hand under her
shirt and gropes the underside of her breast. His index finger grazes a soft nipple. He summons its salmon tone. She
pushes his hand away, shifts position and breaks the connection. Mort rolls the opposite way and dishevels the covers.

"Squeaky's husband is a stock broker. Maybe you could go
back to school and get a job like that."

"A stockbroker? I want to get a job, Honey, but one more
suited to my personality. A stockbroker? Who've you
lived with all these years? A stranger? A stockbroker?"

"You haven't worked in a year. You have to get a job Mort.
We can't survive much longer."

"I said I'd get a job, what more do you want?"

"I want you to get a job."

She cries too quickly. Maybe the tears had started before
he came in. Mort stares up at the ceiling fan. The frozen
blades wait for the next heat wave to lend purpose. A

subtle light penetrates the window, afterbirth of the city glow. Thirty thousand street lamps illuminate the sleepy necropolis.

"Do you wanna do it?"

"What?"

"Make love."

"Are you crazy?"

"We haven't had sex in a month."

"I can't get into it when my life isn't going right."

"I don't understand."

"That's the problem. My little boy hates where he lives, I hate where I live and the person who's supposed to support us refuses to do anything. No sex with you. No!"

"What does that have to do with it?"

Her whole body is consumed, as with fire, by the frustrated outpouring of emotion.

"You remember that magazine article, in Cosmo. It said men communicate through sex. You're always after me to communicate. I need to communicate. I'm better motivated when I communicate."

She pulls the covers over her shoulder. Mort reaches his hand through the dark to stroke her hair. Her hair was the part of her she'd always felt most confident about—cut straight from the pages of Cosmopolitan magazine.

Mort touches her wet face and she lets out a sleep-agitated gasp. Why should his needs surpass hers? He brings his finger to his own lips to taste the saline and hopes some empathy and maybe tears of his own might come. What a genuine painting it would make! An image of a woman prostrated in the caliginous darkness collapsed into a face full of tears. He could use periwinkle, a palette of grays. Maybe steal a few strokes from Goya, Munch or Manet or Hopper. His dad always liked Hopper. His hand strokes her hair and soothes small gathered groups with quick rhythmic pulls. As the hand slips down onto her breast again, guided by some sex-starved automatic pilot, cock and balls at the controls, Angora whirls like a cyclone out of the sea.

"Don't fucking touch me!"

Eight nails rake Mort's face. A bevy of scratches crescendo into slaps. She screams and pounds him. "You bastard!" Her slashing fingers lock onto his mop-like brown hair and excise a chunk by the root, a carrot harvested. It shakes loose with a patch of skin like a bloody divot. He thinks of Artemisia Gentileschi, of Mishima as St.

Sebastian. The barrage of slaps joined by furious flailing kicks. He can take it but her knee catches his chin as he balls up. The tooth SNAP breaks across the room like a wave on the rocks. As he's falling back, off the bed, his neck whiplashing with the force of the knee blow, her opposite leg collides with his scrotal sac. Mort groans, falls to the floor. "Get out! Get the fuck out!" One last slap punches his nose like a panic button. Other guttural screams of raw rage follow. He's satisfied. A tear wells up behind one red eye.

# TWO

Across town, as Phil and Lilli Tod lock up the Death Museum, the voices of conventioneers spill out of the sidewalk cafés along 5th Avenue. The suits in the bar next to the museum swirl colorful plastic spears in their martinis and puff trendy cigars.

The sleepy Gaslight Quarter is abuzz with political delegates, their protestors and the media. A spectacle is being created for the people watching on tv at home. The difference between the political opinions of each group may be vast, but the difference between the bars and the types of alcohol each group consumes is nominal. Pulling back, each group shares tactics, boasts exploits, lies about conquests, dishes gossip, expounds on sport and tests pick up lines. Some of them tell jokes, though a good third will only get a joke if it's dirty.

As little as fifteen years ago, strippers danced in storefront peep shows up and down the block. The prostitutes that worked the sailor bars and walked the streets have been pushed into the East County and into the barrio near the Naval base.

Senator Dollard, candidate for president, sleeps across the bay in a fancy hotel. The less fancy hotels on Fifth, which once rented rooms by the hour, have been converted to loft live/work spaces for 'Artists.'

In the late 70s and early 80s, the local punks started calling the city "Slow Death" since there wasn't much to do other than cadge cigarettes or fish beers in front of 7-11. At this hour, there's still not much to do in Slow Death other than get drunk. When a 50-year-old man comes out of a restaurant in the center of the city with a 20-year-old blonde on his arm, noting the heels, the legs, the ass etc., it seems obvious she's a paid escort. He'll offer $300 for an hour of "sex-like activity" in his hotel room, so, despite the assurances of the DRC (Downtown Redevelopment Committee), the neighborhood hasn't changed.

A tenebrious pair of 20-year-old frat boys perch on barstools in a café next to the museum. Since neither their cheap suits nor fake IDs were good enough to get them a drink, they puff the trendy cigars and scrutinize their older mentors with envy.

A girl, probably a waitress on her way home from work, doesn't look in their direction when one of them shouts "Woo!"

"We had a good day."

PT, as he's known, scratches the skin on the back of his neck and exposes, briefly, the tattoo which matches the one on Lilli's neck under her thick red hair. After a two-week courtship, the "Arrows of Chaos" proved the perfect choice to symbolize their union.

Lilli doesn't feel awake until the early evening magic hour when the street lamp and neon glow from the bar stoke a subtle aura of thrill through her red hair. When she looks good, she feels good. The black disks of her eyes shy away from the noonday sun, which even through the gloom, feels too bright.

PT chuckles.

"Every day's a good day for a Heiny!" He takes the last swig and sets the green bottle inside the door before shutting it.

"I better drive home."

"Fuck that."

Lilli hesitates to argue with PT, which can feel like boxing a circus kangaroo.

"Who was that guy you were yelling at?"

"Some braindead dude with a military haircut kicked Stella."

"What the fuck are you doing bro? Show some respect for the dead."

"I didn't know it was taxidermy, I thought the dog was alive."

How the box cutter came to be in PT's hand, the man who kicked the dog couldn't say. He could say the hand was steady and held even with PT's black and unblinking doll's eyes.

"You'd kick a live dog!"

"I told him to get down on his knees."

The frightened customer complies, careful not to make hasty movements.

"Lay down." PT gives him a swift kick in the gut which causes the frightened man to tremble.

"After that, I told him to get the fuck out!"

"You shouldn't treat the customers like dogs."

"Fuck that, dogs are better than people."

"PT, please, there are a lot of cops out tonight."

A black and white police cruiser stops at the traffic light. "Protect and Serve" painted on the door.

"No worries Lil, I got my get outta jail free card!"

Cops like to hang around the Death Museum, desensitizing themselves for the hardscrabble reality of their jobs. Mort, whenever he picks up a shift, feels "totally paranoid, totally aware" whenever the gun and badge strut down the stairs. Wherever he is in the city, he feels nervous when a black and white pulls up behind him. At the museum, he feels like a convict looking through the bars with a little mirror. *Understand we're fighting a war, we can't win…* The cops seem to get off on the El Salvadoran snuff video which plays on a loop in the museum's little theater in between news items about the famous fatal car crashes of Jane Mansfield, Grace Kelly, Eddie Cochrane, Marc Bolan, Jackson Pollock, Albert Camus, D. Boon, Sam Kinison, Billy Martin, Clifford Brown, Stiv Bators… and the infamous "Train Video." Living vicariously, they take mental note of the death squads' barbarous tactics, biding time until the inevitable "Day the Gloves Come Off."

Many of the grisly photographs displayed in the museum were taken by cops and firefighters—wipeouts, crime scenes, car wrecks… A firefighter came in while Mort was working and said permission to take pictures out in the field had been revoked.

> "This family stopped by the station to thank us for cleaning up after their son. There was a picture of his scrambled brains tacked to the bulletin board. That was the end of that."

PT waves the orange Monopoly card with the chief's signature in Lilli's face. A quick snatch sees the card tucked between her cleavage under the baby-doll Slayer tee.

"How 'bout your get-out-of-the-hospital free card, hmm?"

As soon as PT turns the deadbolt, a bony white finger taps his shoulder. Their landlord. PT and Lilli refer to him as

"Slumlord" (to his face of course) since he doesn't care that the roof leaks or that rats run rampant through the basement.

"Slumlord, you here for the rats?"

"The rats give this place an edge. Hee hee hee."

Lilli takes a step back. The old man smells loathsome, like he sucked on mothballs to relieve a sore throat. The musty old boat smell reminds her of the basement. She imagines cancer eating his prostate, pictures a skeleton with its hand out for the rent.

"Hee hee heh. I came to talk about business. How's business?"

He seems to have had a minor stroke since the last time they saw him, some of the muscles in his face have stiffened. His deadpan voice reminds Lilli, in a way, of Bill Burroughs reading one of his routines.

> "…*venerable honored men surrendered themselves to the embraces of a lecherous, snarling simian.*"

"Slumlord, why do you always ask about business? It's not good for your heart. Try 'How's life' or 'How's it going?'"

"Miserable, brutish and short. A bit of a cruel question to ask at my age, eh Lilli?"

"It's the one everybody asks at death's door."

The landlord utters a bouquet of subsonic grunts before he repeats his query about business.

"Business is okay."

"I watched from across the street, hee hee hee. From the shoeshine stand. I own that side of the block too you know? I counted forty-seven customers. Forty-seven at five bucks a head. With that kind of flow, I'd say you were better than okay. In fact, you're making a killing, hee hee heh. Oh… and… a punk with a black trench coat shoplifted a postcard off your rack there. You gotta watch those little shit eating fucktards. Ha ha ha…And the squid! Ha. In his civvies shook his fist and cursed in your general direction. Hee heh. You better watch your backs."

PT tries to ferret out the old miser's intentions.

"It's the convention. Republicans love death."

"I have to raise the rent on you folks. I don't want to do it, but the cost of living is up, up, up. Inflation, taxes. Goddam taxes. Your lease expires next month. Fair warning. I gave fair warning."

PT stares with a snarl that indicates his mood has flipped from bountiful to pestilent. He'd like to punch the old man in his bony face. His body tenses and twenty eyes from a variety of tattooed creatures on his arms acquire a harder gaze. He never liked the landlord, but thought

$1,600 a month was a square deal. He was a capitalist himself, after all.

"I've got to get $4,800 for this space."

"That's triple what we pay!"

PT remains cool and silent.

"I need the money Lilli. It's not personal. If your sicko museum can't generate the revenue, we'll bring in Starbucks or McDonald's. The neighborhood's going that way. Up, up, up."

A small Native American craft shop down the block, that sold turquoise jewelry, dream catchers and kachina dolls, closed its doors at the beginning of the month. The word on the street augurs Burger King opening a themed craft brewery with "Have it Your Way IPA" and "Whopper Stout" on tap. Ten years back, 548 5th Avenue was a pool hall. Before that a hotel. Before that a brothel. Before that a Turkish bath. Before that a mortuary. Before that a furniture shop. Before that a field. Before that an ocean…

PT remains silent. The landlord tips his beat fedora, which exposes skin on his bald head so thin the lumpy casement shines through underneath. Lilli, usually the calm one, throws a second-degree murderous look at him, but PT's grim reserve lends restraint. As the old man walks away, he seems to dissolve into the night like a ghost up from hell. Into thin air.

Two uniformed cops ride up on bicycles.

"Hey PT, hello Lilli."

"You guys closed up for the night?"

PT hands Lilli the car keys as she swallows her disgust and nods in the affirmative. The small museum curators stand on the sidewalk in front of their shop reflecting on a life-time of artifact collection. The heinous deeds of their mur-derous benefactors flash off the walls into their minds—Richard Speck, Henry Lee Lucas, Charles Manson, Ted Bundy, Lawrence Bittaker, David Berkowitz, Richard Ramirez, John Wayne Gacy.

For a second, the couple entertain the idea of joining the ranks, but only for a second.

## THREE

There's a BUZZING. It could be a chain saw or a fallen bee-hive. It could be an elevator emergency or a diesel truck backing up or a jet taking off. It could be a baby crying. It could be an alarm clock decrying 6am.

The deadened sun gathers behind the shade that protects the window. One red eye opens. Mort's wife is supposed to go to work. He's naked, covered by the red and black crocheted blanket Angora put out to hide a stain on the couch. The first sense of stiffness is in his neck. His skin registers a chill. His wife, usually petite, looms overhead.

"Are you awake?"

"Mmm. TOOOT."

Mort isn't ready for speech, not unusual for morning. He makes a strange whistling sound.

"I had the most bizarre dream last night…" She tells it in minute prosaic detail though he's not ready to listen. She throws in something that happened between Cubby and a friend at school, talking fast like she's already drunk too much coffee. He gets confused, unsure which part happened in the netherworld of her dreams.

"Uhh."

"You need to get Cubby ready for school. He'll need breakfast and you have to pack a lunch."

"Yeah, okay. TOOOT. I didn't sleep good. 'The Bat Signal' kept waking me up. TOOOT."

Mort's blue eyes refuse to open. And there's that whistle again. Weird. A crusty mortar seals the eyes and in his next moment of consciousness a door shuts and locks from the outside. He falls into a hazy torpor and has his own dream about three large shoes, like some sad-faced Ringling Brothers clown from 1910 might wear, arranged in a triangle around a menacing wad of chewed pink bubblegum.

Angora climbs into a beat-up Toyota station wagon. She puts the key in the ignition. Turns it. She remembers the new starter button, installed to bypass the neutral safety switch; a broken part of the car that, apparently, would have cost two-hundred to replace, while the jury-rigged button was fifty. So, the car starts like a doorbell.

The upholstery has peeled back with time and since the foam rubber ripped, her lower back presses against the wire frame of the seat. Cars like people revert to skeleton form—rust has already eaten the outer shell near the hatchback spreading like the hole in the ozone layer over Chile. She depresses the button and the engine chugs, shudders ready for action. The windows are fogged. The defroster doesn't work and forget the heater. She speeds off toward the freeway.

"Uhhh. This car is not safe. I'm gonna die. If I get stuck somewhere, Mort's dead meat."

She reaches to turn on the FM radio and notices that it's missing. Gone. Stolen. When was the last time she listened?

"What the…?"

The thieves removed the stereo cassette player and installed an old model 8-track. Most likely a prank by Mort's friends from art school. The 8-Track poking out the mouth with sun-faded letters is by Del Shannon.

A memory of her parents' station wagon, a trip across two states, with an 8-Track version of The Mormon Tabernacle Choir. She pushes the tape into the play position and Shannon sings:

> *As I walk along, I wonder, what went wrong with our love…*

Around nine, Cubby climbs out of bed and 'hops on pop' startling Mort awake. His eyes feel less glued, the light in the room feels more intense.

"Eh slugger, what's happening in dreamland. TOOOT."

"I'm hungry Dad. What's that funny toot noise?"

Some parents spare their kids adult problems, but Mort doesn't believe in censorship. The cat is out of the barn. Cubby is already on the inexorable frog march from innocence to experience. And truth can hurt like a kick in the mouth, but what is the truth here? Just because it isn't easy, doesn't mean there isn't any.

"Your mother hit me with her knee, on accident, and broke my tooth. TOOOT."

The little boy lets out a series of laughs, each building in intensity.

"Laugh eh? I'll give you something to laugh about. TOOOT."

Mort tickles the little boy without mercy. He continues tickling until tears and stops just shy of a bladder release, grabbing his son in a headlock to rub a sore spot on the boy's head with a knuckle.

"I'm sorry Dad, hee hee hee."

"Who's the king? TOOOT."

"You are, you are."

"Who's the toady bootlicking sycophant? TOOOT."

"I am."

Mort releases his grip. Cubby jumps onto the arm of the couch and bounds to the coffee table.

"You are. You are. You're the toady bootlicking psychophant."

The boy cuts down the hall. Mort stands up, aware of several bones he took for granted, courtesy of last night's drubbing. He feels over his swollen lip into the oblivion of his broken tooth.

"You wanna eat, get yourself some cereal. TOOOT."

Mort plods to the kitchen one step at a time. He opens the refrigerator—sees a blur of foodstuffs. He forgets coffee is his mission. He shuts the refrigerator. His blue eyes pan the room. The espresso machine! A jack-o-lantern grin lights across his face.

Mort opens the fridge again. Milk, pitcher of orange juice, mustard… coffee beans! He lifts the bag of ground beans. He huffs on the bag. The rich dark tones of the coffee enter his lungs. The smell of fresh ground espresso brings delight to his aching body. He sets the bag down, lifts the arm of the home espresso machine and walks to the kitchen door. Birds sing outside on the wire—none too flamboyant, a pair of baleful dun-colored mourning doves. A barren tree sways in a light breeze. The sun is diffused, but bright through a dingy sheet of high clouds.

He dumps yesterday's grounds into the ravine between his building and the neighbor's fence—a space wide enough for a boy to scoot through runs the length of the building. He has dumped grounds here for five years, so a layer of coffee topsoil fills the space. The compacted used coffee grounds retain the form of the machine as they fall. Mort finds some pleasure as he watches the puck plummet through space before exploding in the goal; when the grounds are hot the impact releases a tiny puff of steam. Like *Stukas over Disneyland* sending a family of large brown roaches scurrying for cover. If I was a roach that's where I'd live. Far from the exterminator's ever-watchful eye. Emperor of the grounds, king of the coffee mound.

Cubby stands on a chair and reaches for a bowl in the cupboard. The cereal is on the counter and a jug of fat free milk. Mort returns to the business of making coffee. It's past time for school to start.

"Hey, Tiger, what do you say we take a mental health day. TOOOT."

Cubby does a little dance. His feet pump like a humming-bird's wings.

"Yes!"

Father and son clap hands in a high five which flows into a deep bear hug.

"I thought we could go down to the thrift store and see if they had any of the board games I had when I was a kid. TOOOT."

The department stores are marketing many of the games Mort played with for a new generation. He marvels at how his parents could afford all this plastic crap. Stretch Armstrong, Magic 8-ball, Break the Ice, Gnip-Gnop, Rock 'Em Sock 'Em Robots, Operation, Risk, Life, Clue, Trouble. The inexplicable disposable wages of the two-income family. Mort remains in his zombie half-sleep, trying to wake up, as he waits for the espresso. He continues to hold on to his son as the machine hisses and spits out the black liquid fuel of the morning.

Mort empties a load of piss into the toilet. Technically, he shoots at the toilet, but some of the piss sprays sideways out his morning penis and wets the tile. He's been trained to lift the lid and the wife thinks she can teach him to piss straight, as she tries to teach her son, but there is no accountability for the randomness of that first morning piss, which might take flight in any of eight directions.

The urine in the bowl looks like it has blood in it. He recalls the shot he took in the balls. Feels the blow in his stomach. Angora installed one of those blue Sani-Flush deodorizers, so the artist blends the yellow piss, weird electric blue water and russet red blood into a soupy mahogany.

If it's yellow, let it mellow. If it's brown… WHOOSH.

He stares at a face in the mirror. The landscape has shifted, like the shape of the beach after a storm. A sand dune in the wind. His lip is swollen, blue. Four red roads streak down his cheek and continue on the upper part of his chest. His wife tore him up. His greasy hair looks like a bomb blast. It mushrooms in an impossible-to-tame cloud. He pats at it, picks up a comb, puts the comb down. Fuck it. The missing divot, scabbed over, stings to the touch.

The caput-mortuum-colored rings around his eyes are of a hue Chardin might have used. He played a tough game and lost.

He files it in the catalog of minor injuries collected over a life. People who take the time to look at him sometimes ask if he's wasted, which would explain a lot, though most people get stuck in the clear lake blue at the center of his eyes.

He tried alcoholism for a few months, which left no more lasting impression than constructivism, fauvism, existentialism, nihilism or futurism. His pro and con list had notches on both sides. He dug the floaty feel of the hangover. The massacred, lazy-lost drunken boat feeling at rest all day in bed without purpose. He liked the no-place-to-be feeling because it matched how he felt most of the time. Being hungover was an excuse, to himself, that covered up his natural sloth. Most people run through life so frenetically they fail to simply do nothing.

Nevertheless, he scorned throwing up and despised head-aches, so nausea kept him sober.

Mort picks up his toothbrush, applies a worm of tropical sky-blue paste. He lifts the swollen part of his lip with one finger on his left hand to get a better look at the gap left by the broken tooth. It surprises him, like staring into a black hole in the void of space. He tries to brush around it but when the bristles fleck against the raw broken spot, electric sparks of pain ruminate through his extremities. The pain bumps against his toes and rolls back toward his head ending as a throb in the tooth itself.

The thrift store is downtown, a mile walk from the apart-ment. Mort bought most of his clothes here, except the ones his dad gave for Xmas. In high school he lived in a "mod, mod world" where records by The Jam and The Who taught him how to dress, a way to be. He smoked clove cigarettes and rode around the city on the back of Harold the Mod's Vespa. Someone told him cloves were stuffed with horse shit, which helped him to drop those "coffin nails" though once or twice a year he bums one from that androgynous girl who loiters outside the clubs wearing a parka and cheetah-print brothel creepers. Harry's wife made him sell the Vespa when she found out she was pregnant. He stopped going to shows and disappeared from the scene. So legends fade to nostalgia.

Cubby and Mort walk past a row of street people busy folding their sleep rolls and organizing their possessions in shopping carts. An old woman takes the last pull of last night's wine or as luck would have it, the first pull of the new day's wine. On the freeway overpass, Cubby spots a man in the bushes.

"Dad, that guy's wiping his ass!"

A bald, hairy man stands naked and wipes his ass with a wad of toilet paper. He tucks the filthy tissue into a newspaper, rolls it up and tucks it under his arm. This just above the morning commute, just down the street from the city's financial district, just out of sight from the mayor's office.

Mort has stolen a lot of toilet paper from public toilets. He preys on corporate fast food for condiments, liquid soap and paper towels too. Is it possible to "steal" what is freely given? He walks in, smiles and asks a cashier for the bathroom key. After a crap, he jimmies the lock on the dispenser and stashes the roll in his backpack. He steals by a code, "Never take the last roll or the last drop of soap." He's been carrying empty plastic containers in his backpack since the scouts taught him to "Be prepared." Once he stuck a roll of paper in his boxer shorts which slipped down his pant leg and caused him to walk funny. The hostess barely offered a curious look as he hobbled out to the street.

"Hey, whaddya lookin' at? I'm not some animal in the zoo."

"Hey buddy, why don't you go to Denny's. TOOOT."

"Cause there's no paper in the stall, dude. And if you can't hold it in your hands, you gotta let it go."

Mort and Cubby walk on.

"Why was that man naked, Dad?"

"Well, he'd like some privacy, but he doesn't have a house. TOOOT."

"He could use our bathroom."

"He could… but…there's too many guys like him. This problem is more than we can handle. The city should make bathrooms for people."

"Can we take a dump outside, Dad?"

"Sure. Your mom's friend had to take a dump in a flower pot once on the way home from the bar. It's good to practice. They give you a merit badge for that in the scouts. Be prepared. TOOOT."

Father and son look both ways, cross the trolley tracks and reach the sidewalk. A mannequin in the window of the thrift shop wears summer togs—pink bathing trunks and a red Hawaiian shirt. The window dresser is either color blind or the store is overfished, picked clean by a new generation of punks.

Inside the store, the smell of used clothes irritates the boy's nostrils. Mort walks past a shelf of romance paperbacks into the main room. A sea of dead people's clothes—dead men's suits, dead women's blouses. Even the underwear of the dead hangs around the room. Each aisle topped with a rack of shoes that curl at the toe, soles worn thin, with annihilated arch support, dull flat textures and dirty laces.

Mort draws the line at thrift store shoes, though he buys thrift soccer cleats for Cubby, since kids grow out of shoes before they wreck them.

"Do your soccer cleats still fit? TOOOT."

"Yeah, Dad, they're too big. I always trip on the field."

The cashier's face would make a good painting. It tells a story of a life beaten by hard luck and hard living. She wears a faded navy-blue smock with the name of the thrift shop embossed on the front in ochre yellow. Her attention is focused on a black and white tv with a bent antenna where a grainy Bela Lugosi, in the middle ground between two impromptu grave markers, turns from the camera and wraps himself in a black cape before sashaying off screen.

Mort and Cubby make their way to the children's section. They scan the shelves, look through boxes of puzzles. Cubby finds a Monopoly set missing its bank, closer examination would reveal but six tokens, since the Top Hat absconded with the money and the Metal Dog to a tiny green plastic house under the cushions of a couch on Virginia Avenue in Atlantic City.

The couch was handed down to somebody's children; the poor cushions were so sad and battered the couch was pushed out to the curb. It was picked up in the middle of the night by a family of immigrants who carried it a thousand miles while they chased a better life before they left it for junk. City workers buried it in a field with old tires and rotten bananas.

How the bulk of the game got to this California thrift store is another story—a different book from a different time about the mysterious death of a child murdered, so suspect the FBI, by its own father, walking among us to this day, due, mainly, to a lack of evidence the DA might bring to trial…

"Mouse Trap! TOOOT."

Mort grabs the box from the top shelf. It's taped shut. He shakes it and the plastic parts rattle.

"Mouse Trap Game? Looks crappy. Can we get this old Atari?"

"This is a great game, Cubby. I had it when I was a kid. TOOOT."

Cubby sort of fakes a smile, which his dad fails to notice. Cubby wonders what his friends are up to on the playground. Maybe he should have gone to school.

The lady at the register stares at Mort. She punches in the price.

"That'll be one dollar."

"What? TOOOT."

"No worries dude. Looks like a bad hair day."

She closes the sale with an inappropriate cackle; the scabby patch of missing hair on Mort's scalp itches.

"You watch too much tv lady. Kill your television before it kills you. TOOOT.

## FOUR

A teacher stands in front of a class holding a long-haired rabbit. A few woodchips stick to its fur, others fall back into the cage. The class sits up straight in individual desks with their hands folded across their laps, all these kids look the same—the boys' hair cropped in buzz cuts; the girls' held steady with pink barrettes. President Nixon's photo is framed on the wall under the flag.

"What kind of rabbit is that Ms. Bishop?"

"Angora, can you tell us?"

A tremulous girl with straight brown hair gathered in twin ponytails and a freckled face yet to grow into her front teeth, focuses on the desk rather than the teacher. She mumbles, "I don't know" so quietly the girl one desk to the front can't hear.

The teacher turns to the blackboard and chalks the word A-N-G-O-R-A in dusty white letters. The class laughs at this, which startles the rabbit and induces a skittish stream of yellow piss across the teacher's desk, provoking more uproarious laughter, as if they'd never seen anything so funny. The teacher sops up the urine with a stack of drawings the students made as Angora drops her head on the desk to cry inside a cave of folded arms. The next day little Bobby Harris, whose drunken father beats him savagely with a switch, leaves a carrot on her desk.

This incident haunted her through grade school into junior high as the story went around how "Angora peed in class." That's how it was remembered. A capstone on a series of humiliations that soured her on school. Her parents didn't know why she sulked weekday mornings. Lots of kids didn't like school. Her father had spent a few spring days playing hooky at the fishing hole himself. It was normal.

She fantasized about a protector. A knight, a prince… a big brother to kick Bobby Harris's ass. Her need for a superhero to swoop in fell in line with most Americans. Her mother taught her to cook and clean. Her father taught her that being pretty was important. Her best option, they thought, was marriage.

And then the kids on the street went from playing cops and robbers to tv tag to *Charlie's Angels*, and even though she wasn't allowed to watch it, she could become Kate Jackson, kicking ass and solving crimes.

Her father named her "Angora" after her mother's baby blue sweater. "I saw that sweater across the room and that was it. I was like a worm on a hook." Through grade school, Angora longed for an average name. Teachers said it wrong and it didn't shorten neatly into a quaint sobriquet. Mort was the first person who told her it was unique, beautiful like her autumnal eyes, deep like the kisses they shared at 2am.

Angora stands behind the counter of an espresso bar in the lobby of a hospital. Her smile is contagious. A customer sips a latte—takes a second to breathe while his own smile blooms like nightshade—and stuffs a dollar in the tip jar.

"Damn good coffee."

Angora wants to feel pride in her work, but making coffee isn't on par with the doctors and nurses who race around the halls saving people's lives. She'd like to earn more than minimum wage, so Cubby could grow up in a better neighborhood. She'd love to have another child, but that seems more unlikely every day.

At home, she makes sure Cubby is healthy and safe. She provides nutritious food, washes his clothes. She plans activities to build his self-esteem and makes him do homework. The remuneration for caregiving, they say, is built in. It is its own reward.

Selling coffee at the hospital isn't easy. She has to manage expectations all day, on her feet long enough for them to ache and tie her calf muscles in knots. She listens to problems, ameliorates stress and lightens the burden of grief. She'd make a decent psychologist, if she could get through school. Mort credits her power to feel thoughts and intuit feelings at "Genius Level," though maybe this is another ploy to lower expectations for his inability to really listen.

In junior college, a professor tested her for dyslexia. She had trouble reading and even everyday words were impossible to spell. Her teachers called her lazy. Her parents said she didn't try. She was made to feel stupid until she dropped out of high school. She got pregnant with Cubby in junior college and didn't see herself going back. She would never go back.

"That's a great cup of java."

"Thank you sir."

Considering the quality of the man's suit as he walks away, she turns to her coworker and says in a hushed voice, "So why not leave a tip?"

Somehow, owing to acoustics or a sudden hush falling across the lobby, the man turns back to the bar.

His first impulse is to have the manager place a "Warning" in her file. She should be grateful for this job. The impudent bitch. If she had bigger tits he might have left a tip. When a waitress leans over the table and gives him an ogle of voluptuous fat, he has no problem tucking a dollar under the plate. Tit for tat. As he scrutinizes Angora, his glandular eye scans up and down her body leaving a slimy mucoid residue. He strains at the merciful synapse in his brain to keep from throwing a tantrum. Who did this B-cupped barista think she was?

"Excuse me, Ma'am, but I need this money for bus fare."

She senses the sarcasm and also feels guilty for letting him see her frustration. The feeling in her stomach recalls a chastisement from her mother the one time she let her bra strap show.

"I'm sorry. It—"

The man exits the lobby wearing imported Italian leather shoes and a Rolex that glimmers in the tepid sunlight. He stops to speak with the valet—a 20-year-old blonde endowed by surgery. She'd been a stripper, but the purple scars on her breasts, which had a foul thickness, didn't heal and the manager at the strip club said, "Sorry babe, but those baps are gruesome. All my years in the biz and never such disfigurement." She hoped parking cars could pay off the small business loan on the implants and keep her in her own apartment. She'd sooner get a roommate than move back with her own mother.

The valet grabs the keys and hustles to the garage. A minute later, a gunmetal mica-colored Jaguar slinks up to the curb. The man who didn't tip buffs the hood ornament with a white hankie. The valet slips out of the car, the way actresses fall out of lingerie in movies. Such long slender legs. Mr. 'Taking the Bus', Mr. Liar hands her a dollar. Mr. Rolex. Mr. Jaguar.

At this moment, a whole group of workers burst out of the elevator on their ten-minute break.

"Double latte."

"Single mocha."

"Non-fat cap."

A doctor in green scrubs with an antiviral mask stretched over his face taps a pen on the counter. Angora struggles to fill the orders. She sweats. Her coworker has already been gone 20 minutes on her 15-minute break. Angora feels another man's eyes on her breasts, his tongue tip wet against dry lips. She pushes some of the sweat off her eyebrows with a napkin and hopes her antiperspirant holds.

What is 'aluminum zirconium trichlorohydrex?'

A woman compliments Angora's hair, but seems surprised by the price of her drink so doesn't leave a tip. The next guy tosses in a nickel, two pennies and a piece of lint from his pocket.

After the melee, the tip jar bent the scale at a dollar seven. The bills Angora stuffed in the jar failed to spur donations. Mort's friend Jimenez says, "guilt is a poor motivator," but she'd learned about mirror neurons in a psych class at junior college and thought she could tap the part of the brain that drives emulation with these shills. She gives her coworker fifty-four cents.

Angora sips a vanilla latte, smiles when three customers in a row complain about the wait, the wait, the wait—always friendly, all apologies. To what end.

FIVE

The boys set up the Mouse Trap Game on the dinner table. Four tubes of paint, a pallet and sketch book had to be moved aside. Mort tosses the notebook on top of some opened but ignored mail, a stack of artist bios on Arbus, Gorky, Kahlo & Rivera, Van Gogh's letters, Wojnarowicz's *Close to the Knives*, Gauguin's *Writings of a Savage* and *Secret Exhibitions*...where he first encountered Jay DeFeo's epic painting *The Rose.* He opens the book. This is art. This is a lifelong dedication to art.

For years, Angora has been after Mort to revise his chaotic organization strategy. Maybe she's right, maybe I'd get more done. He opens a drawer and stashes the paint tubes. There's an old brush behind a passel of photographs and a coffee can chuck full of wheat stalk pennies.

The table, an office desk, a red Olivetti typer, two bookshelves and a chartreuse-colored futon couch furnish the "aluminum room" which was added after the 1930 plaster home was built. The tin roof amplifies the summer heat and intensifies the winter chill which makes it too often inhospitable for most humans. It was Death Valley or Siberia in there. Mort would strip naked when it was hot or layer his clothes and wrap himself in a blanket through the winter to avoid the tv and sit out there thinking about art.

"Cubby, put on a sweater. TOOOT."

"Okay Dad."

He spreads a farrago of colorful pieces on the table and after a quick inventory, a few parts seem to be missing.

"What can we use to improvise, Tiger? TOOOT."

"How about a spoon, Dad?"

"Perfect, get a spoon from the kitchen. And a pipe cleaner from the junk drawer. TOOOT."

"Okay Dad."

Cubby skips off. The game uses a series of actions set in motion by a rolling marble which trips a switch to push and pull a series of gadgets until the cage falls on the little plastic mouse. A compendium of cause and effect. Cubby returns to find his dad staring into space.

"What's the matter, Dad?"

"Huh? Oh nothing…TOOOT."

They take their time and assemble the game. Cubby is sent on several trips to the kitchen for extra parts. Mort hands his son the last piece to set in place.

"It's a work of art, Dad."

"You're right. TOOOT."

Artists claim to be inspired by Mahler, Poe, Van Gogh, but real influence also comes from life. Not this childhood toy necessarily, but this moment—when a father and son work together to build a bigger world than themselves. That's where art comes from. From authentic moments. Even hard-sought originality comes second to the real and the true. In art school, Mort built a mechanical sculpture that had no purpose. It was made of brass rods, tiny hinges and pulleys. Perpetual Stasis Machine #002 rested on the dresser above his sock drawer. His teacher wasn't impressed, but the next term he submitted it as a self-portrait and won high marks.

"We should wait for Mom to get home before we run it."

"There's an idea, but what if it ruins itself, maybe we should test it. TOOOT.

The boy shakes his head with a vigorous finality. Mort feels let down. What's with this kid's immutable desire to perform for his mother? "Look mom… look mom… look mom…"

"Dad, when are you going to get a haircut? Mom says you'll never be able to get a job with hair like that."

Mort smiles revealing his broken grin.

"Get the scissors from the bathroom, I'll meet you in the living room. TOOOT."

The boy sprints on another errand.

The louche green chair swivels and rocks. It was the color Manet poured into the glass of the absinthe drinker—a good chair for reading. And Mort spent many hours in it with Dr. Seuss and *Where the Wild Things Are* or singing "hush little baby" songs.

> Hush little baby don't say a thing
> Daddy's going to buy you diamond ring
> And if that diamond ring turns to glass
> Daddy's gonna kick the guy-who-sold-it-to-him's ass

When Cubby fit in the crook of daddy's arm, Mort would read aloud from *Twilight of the Idols*. He drags the chair to the center of the room and it scrapes along the scuffed wood floor. Cubby appears from the bathroom with scissors gripped in his left hand. His dad recognizes the excitement on his son's face.

He puts The Cramps into the CD player, cranks up the volume as Lux Interior blurts,

> *I'm a human fly and I don't know why.*

He remembered the day his best friend Jimenez shaved his head—'bzz bzz bzz'—to this same tune in 1985. They'd gotten drunk on generic beer and saw D.O.A. at Wabash Hall.

Cubby sets the scissors on the table. He grips one end of a white bed sheet and flips it over his dad, a do-it-yourself Halloween ghost. Cubby seizes the opportunity to execute a playful flying tackle and Mort rolls off the chair onto the floor with the sheet covering his outstretched body.

"Alright. Alright."

Cubby digs into his father's ribs and tickles him.

"Ha ha, I surrender. TOOOT."

Mort surges up and catches his son in the sheet. In one big motion, he deadlifts the boy like a full diaper or sack of animated laundry.

"Let's do this haircut. TOOOT."

"Right-e-o Daddy-o."

Cubby giggles and picks up the scissors as Mort, swivels in the green chair and readjusts the sheet-wrap.

"Okay, Barber, take it all off. TOOOT."

"All of it?"

"All. TOOOT."

Cubby has a huge smile on his face, revealing his own lost tooth. After the fiasco with Elmo, he hadn't expected another chance to play barber. He was five and thought his hair would grow back. It didn't.

Virginia Woolf, who filled her pockets with stones and walked into a river, said, in *Orlando*, we "lose some illusions," as we grow up, "perhaps to acquire others."

Cubby grips the scissors and clips one greasy dark lock at a time. The boy works ardently and imagines he's in a barber shop. He wishes he had more tools. The different-sized combs soaking in that jar of blue liquid. The old gray lotions. The clippers that vibrate. A brush for the talcum powder and three or four flavors of lollipop to hand out at his discretion.

"What do you think about the Padres next season? Caminiti should hit a lot of homers…"

In Mort's fantasy barber shop, there will be no small talk. Idle chit-chat crossing a patron's mind, shouldn't cross his lips. The music rules, as the straight razor flashes about a man's throat. Banter is ill-advised this close to the jugular. "Action Coiffure" is about rhythm, gesture and movement. Symmetry is for scientists and aesthetes. Our school wants emotional response, gut reaction and a delayed sense of ache that hits you like walking over the next rise to find your hometown set ablaze.

Mort spins the chair to show his victim a new haircut. Smiling to reveal his broken grin, he asks, "What do you feel?" After "Automatic Clipping," a new-bald hippie bears his auburn curls from the bier in an infant's casket to face the future. When a businessman needs a trim before the big meeting, the bouncer at the gate will say, "Mohawk this guy." Fraternity Brothers! Step right up. Today's special is 80% off! ¡Enigma! ¡Alarma! ¡Horrendo! His stupefied victims yowl like alley cats after a fight with chunks of fur gouged away in fury.

"Ow. Go easy on the sore spot. TOOOT."

Cubby tries to clip more gently around the scab on his father's head. As Mort slips back into the daydream, Cubby butchers, hacks at and pulls the hair or cuts too close to the skull.

The boys are so caught up in the game of barber they don't hear the key in the lock. They don't hear the door swing open. They don't feel her presence in the room.

"What are you knuckleheads up to?"

Cubby whips the scissors behind his back, "Nothing Mom." There's hair all over the floor. Mort's head looks like a civil war battlefield. A truly punk rock haircut. An abstract sculpture.

"Cubby's giving me a haircut, so I can get a job. TOOOT."

Mort smiles revealing his broken grin. Angora surveys the damage. Any anger dissolves into pathos. Mort catches a glimpse of himself reflected on the tv screen.

"Ay caramba! TOOOT."

Angora laughs and holds a hand out for the scissors.

"Let me cut some."

"Mom, I'm the barber."

Her gaze enforces compliance. The eight-year-old boy hands over the scissors. She works to even it out, until Mort's head looks like a dog-chewed tennis ball.

"The parts that were cut to bald will grow out in a few days."

"Dad said I could take a mental health day."

"You didn't go to school?"

"We went to the thrift store and bought a mousetrap."

"A mousetrap. Eeeek. We have mice? I can't live with mice. I refuse to live with mice."

"No, Mom, it's a game. Come and watch us set it off. Come on. Come on!"

Angora looks at Mort who sweeps the clipped locks of greasy brown hair.

"I need to take a shower."

When Cubby's face sags a little forlorn, neither parent seems to notice. The ridiculous haircut dominates his mom's thoughts. His dad pushes hair into the dustpan and jams a Dead Boys CD into the player.

Mort holds the broom like a guitar and bangs down hard on the first chords. As his father picks at the riff, the boy sets his sulk to the side and hits three percussive blows on the air drums.

Father and son growl along with Stiv Bators:

> *…I got my time machine, my electronic dream. Sonic reducer. Ain't no loser.*

"Check it out, family, it's a brand-new dance. TOOOT."

They ride the pony and sweep and do the twist and brush off rogue hairs and mix the swim with the alligator wildly in time to the painkiller music.

Angora retreats to the bathroom.

"Take out the trash and finish cleaning your room, kid. TOOOT."

"Sure thing Pops."

The little boy pogos off with a bag of hair.

Mort ambles down the hallway and eases open the bathroom door. Angora is stripping off her uniform. Her bare feet leave perspiration kisses on the tile.

"I'm sorry. TOOOT."

Angora studies his face, thinks about the whistle and the broken tooth.

"Can you check the shower for roaches?"

He pulls the shower curtain. Ready to catch any roach he comes across and drop it onto the coffee mound outside. He'd like to mark its exoskeleton, with paint, to see if the same one climbs back into the house.

"Clear. What happened at work? TOOOT."

Angora stands in unmatched bra and panties, needs new underwear.

"Nothing. Some jerky customer."

To Mort's surprise, Angora unbuttons his trousers. Three fingers pull out his penis, which doubles in size like an inflatable raft or one of those compacted sponges set in water. She kneels down and kisses it. He leans against the door, it feels cold. His cock slides into her mouth. He concentrates on the surprise blow job as her front teeth scrape the head.

"I love you and I want our family to stay together. TOOOT."

"I know."

"You've been in every way all anyone could be."

The cock slides in but he has to cum so pulls out to watch the fish-belly white semen purl into the palm of his hand. His erection dies its little death and recedes like one of those Shrinky Dinks toys you cook in the oven.

Angora steps into the steamy shower.

"Go check on Cubby."

Mort saunters down the hall with a pep in his stride.

Angora lets the hot water caress her body. What bizarre mojo swayed her to put Mort's unwashed penis in her mouth? Guilt. I shouldn't have hit him like that. She opens her mouth and the water flushes out the residual taste, short term memory dissipates in steam. The heat and the pressure of the water feel good against her skin.

Mort drives in silence to pick up a pizza for dinner. At the restaurant, he ignores the tip jar next to the register and adds a bottle of root beer and a neon green grapefruit-flavored Jarritos before paying with a fistful of Angora's tip money. His body aches.

Cubby seems more excited about "Pizza Night" than either of his parents. He mixes the root beer with the grapefruit drink in a glass and adds a little orange juice and milk from the fridge. Mort sets the pizza on the coffee table and they take positions around it. Angora tells the story about the customer and her faux pas.

"Mr. Jaguar totally lied to me."

"That sucks."

"He was probably having a bad day, but that's no reason to be rude. Ha ha. He totally 'Ma'amed' me."

"Cubby and I could've followed the rat fink home and took a shit on his doorstep. TOOOT."

Cubby laughs with pizza in his mouth.

"Mort."

"We could put a dead fish in his car or run a hose through his mail slot. TOOOT."

"Mort."

"Oh, oh! Leave a special carton of milk out of the fridge for a few days and if he comes back, make his drink with it. TOOOT."

"Mort, stop."

"Mom, we saw a naked man under a bridge today."

"Hey, let's fire off the mousetrap. TOOOT."

"Yeah, yeah, yeah."

The hours since its construction have given the game more buildup than it deserves. Cubby pulls his mom by the hand into the aluminum room. The mousetrap stands as they left it in all its plastic glory. Angora recognizes parts of the game from childhood and other parts from the kitchen.

"Isn't that our garlic press?"

"Yeah Mom, we needed it."

Mort adjusts one of the pieces.

"Okay Cubby, let her rip. TOOOT."

The little boy lets the marble roll. The sphere moves along a track and collides with a doohickey which releases a spring… Mort watches with each breath contingent on every action and reaction. Cubby's face glows. Even Angora smiles as the pieces trip and BOINK with quantum precision. In the end, the cage traps the mouse to everyone's delight and in a way preserves a family for another day.

SIX

Angora calls at 8:59am to make sure Cubby got to school.
Mort leans back in the green chair and rubs his hand over
his bald head.

"I dropped him off… I'm headed out to look for a job.
TOOOT."

"You have to fix that tooth. The whistle is too much.
Maybe now you'll see what I mean about insurance being
a necessity. I have to go, bye–"

A throng of caffeine junkies have come begging for their
morning fix.

"Medical insurance is a luxury most Americans can't afford––."

Mort skates through his morning coffee ritual, clap,
dump, WOOOOOOO. He whistles through his broken
tooth gap venturing to control the rush of air. If I can
master it, I can stop this annoying "tooot" or at least add a
musical lilt. He sips the espresso and stares off the bal-
cony. He thinks about jerking off.

Mort revels in coffee as the morning fog peels off the
downtown office towers.

In less than an hour, Mort hikes down First Avenue into
the midst of the modestly tall buildings. He crosses over

the same freeway overpass. The old naked bum isn't in the foliage. He sets a roll of toilet paper on the wall and walks on. Mort pokes his head into the Cuban Cigar Factory where a serious and deliberate man sits in the window and hand rolls the tobacco. He enquires about a "Help Wanted" sign and asks how much the job pays. He jots down the facts in his notebook. He asks about jobs at Lucky's Tattoo parlor on Seventh and the Ye Olde Bike Shoppe on Fifth. He sits at the bus stop bench on Market near Sixth and sketches an idea for a painting.

When Mort hears the city bus coming up the street, he gets up and walks on before it makes an unnecessary stop. He looks in shop windows. He studies a businessman's face for the secret to his financial success and decides he must not worry about fucking people over. Money makes Mort feel impotent. He couldn't sell a life preserver to a foundering millionaire. Couldn't or wouldn't. Frustrated with the lack of instant opportunity, he pops over to the Death Museum to visit PT and Lilli.

Mort worked for them for two weeks, when business was booming with the buzz in every hipster's ear. "Have you been to the Death Museum, I heard they have a baseball autographed by Manson…" It was the best job Mort ever had. His compensation included a six-pack of Heineken left each night in a small refrigerator behind the electric chair, which Mort drank alone or shared with the oddball regulars who hung about the place. Lilli cooked her signature soufflé for occasions and always had simpler fare, like pasta, on hand for any who were hungry.

He presses his face on the window and fogs it up.

Lilli, poised at the ticket counter with one ear on the phone, gestures for him to enter. The hammer whacks that emanate from the basement must be PT installing a new exhibit. A heavy piece of furniture slides across the floor followed by the sound of a power drill boring out a hole.

Lilli has a silver hoop through her nose and a live iguana on her shoulder.

"Hey Mort, dig this nut I've got on the phone." She holds her hand over the mouthpiece. "He read about the museum in People Magazine and wants us to help him commit suicide."

Intrigued, he gestures for Lilli to hand over the phone. "Hold on one second sir." Lilli presses her hand harder. "He's serious."

"Hello, this is Mort Zazuzay, Death Museum Suicide Department. How can I help you? TOOOT."

Lilli constricts her core abdominal muscles to suppress laughter. She talks to "weirdos" every day at the museum, embraces and loves each one, true to the maxim from

Browning's 1932 film *Freaks* which hangs on a banner over the long, narrow hall, *One of us! One of Us!*

Or as PT likes to say, "If you can't join em, kill em and eat em."

"I don't want to live anymore," the voice over the phone says. "I can't."

"Have you reached out to Jack Kevorkian? TOOOT."

"He's not in the phone book. Can you get me his number?"

"Lilli, do we have Kevorkian's number? TOOOT."

"We can't give it out."

A reproduction of Kevorkian's painting *A Very Still Life* hangs on the wall over her left shoulder between prints of de Graag's *Memento Mori* and a painting by Jeanne Hébuterne, who in 1920 chased death out of a window in an act of agonizing self-defenestration.

Lilli sets the iguana on the counter; its claws skitter for traction. She twists a finger up in her red hair with one hand and strokes the iguana with the other.

"No sir, we don't have access to the number. TOOOT."

"I don't have a problem killing myself. That's taken care of. A quick and easy death. What I need is someone to write a suicide note for me and handle the details."

"Suicide note. TOOOT."

Mort smiles revealing his broken grin. Lilli hangs on every word and wishes she had a second line to listen in on, but feels blessed she doesn't have to deal with this kook.

"Yes, I'm sure we could write the note. I would need to ask a few questions. TOOOT."

"What would it cost?"

The gears in Mort's brain turn. Cost? Money? Angora will be happy when I dump a fistful of dosh on the table.

"We work on a sliding scale. Our fees are based on your ability to pay. Of course, a longer note will cost more, for our time you understand. TOOOT."

"It should be articulate, to the point."

"Of course, would you like to get together here at the museum or conduct the whole thing over the phone? TOOOT."

Mort has adopted a funereal tone. He is suddenly a crackerjack businessman and negotiates with the geezer on the line like a pro, with the tact and decorum of a clammy-palmed undertaker. Lilli's first impulse is to veto the guy coming to the museum. On second thought, he might pay to see the exhibits. Five bucks is five bucks.

"I was hoping for a quick form letter."

"In that case, you'll have to call someone else. That isn't what we do. We try to make things more personal. TOOOT."

"Could you make a house call? I don't get out these days. My home might give you a better idea about me than I could express in words."

"House call? Why yes, DMSD takes pride in outreach to our customers. TOOOT."

Mort pulls a face at Lilli, who digs every word. He gestures a scribble and Lilli pushes a pen and notepad across the counter. Mort writes down the address.

"Thank you sir. I'll see you at noon. TOOOT."

"Mort, you are not going to this freak's house."

As Lilli says this, Mort can't help focusing on the taxidermy mice suspended from the ceiling on lines of string. One of the mice has been outfitted with a tiny harp, halo and angel wings. The other has tiny horns glued to his dried and cured fur. Mort's gaze washes over entomological species dried, pinned and displayed—a death's head hawk moth, a scorpion. He pets poor old Stella and surveys the jars of animal testicles preserved in formalde-hyde—cat balls, bat balls, dog balls, human balls. Neatly labeled: Not for sale.

Mort laughs out loud about Lilli's use of the word 'freak.'

"This sounds like the business opportunity I need. If I get paid to write this guy a suicide note, we might make some real cash. I could work out of the back room, set up an office. TOOOT."

He stands lost in thought, a fire burning behind his eyes. Fate called and he answered with the ease of answering the dinner bell or the telephone. He composes the note in his mind while heavy boot steps sound on the stairwell. PT appears with a green glass bottle in one hand.

"Hey bro, what's going on?"

"I just talked to some old guy who wants to kill himself. TOOOT."

"We get calls like that all the time."

"You do? That's great! TOOOT."

"Mort plans to write a suicide note for the guy."

"Get him to do it on video, we can show it down in the museum."

"Maybe he'll leave his skeleton to us in a will. How much would it cost to get the bones cleaned up? TOOOT."

"If you get the right mortician $1,000. The chemicals are cheap. It's a matter of taking the time to clean each bone. It would be best to let the beetles at it for a few months."

"Ob-La-Di Ob-La-Da…"

"Another five hundred to get the bones wired together right. In the end unless the skeleton is famous you're better off finding one used or going with mummification."

"Mummification isn't cheap either, but people will pay to see a mummy."

"You have to find someone with the know-how. Good mummification is expensive."

"A lot of universities are doing it now."

Mort's left brain registers the factoid barrage while his right composes the suicide note and incorporates his new company.

"Mort, on the phone you said… DSM—what was that?"

"DMSD. Death Museum Suicide Division. TOOOT."

PT picks up the iguana and lets it rest on his shoulder. Lilli whistles and a giant pig, who they call Bedlam, galumphs from the back of the room where he'd been asleep in the shadows. He's fully tusked; Lilli has crimson sores on her ankles from constant incidental pokes. Mort's hand brushes the pig's rough hairy skin.

"How much would it cost to get a real Suicide Assistance business up and running? TOOOT."

"You'll run into legal problems."

"I'm not suggesting we kill people. I'd like to avoid the legal system. You know, take care of the details, do the paperwork, death certificates, obits. TOOOT."

"We already have a computer. I guess it would depend on how we advertise."

"You could put up flyers at the Hemlock Society."

"Maybe I could moonlight at the suicide hotline. TOOOT."

"Your face on billboards. 'Feeling low? Lay your fears to rest. 1(888) SUI-CIDE.'"

"You could put up flyers on the bridge next to the sign that says, 'We Care.'"

The entrepreneurs laugh; Mort's broken tooth gapes like a dark abyss.

"We need extra income. Slumlord raised the rent."

"That sucks. You have a lot invested here. Let me go out and see what this guy offers and we'll split the money. You guys bring the business; I'll write the notes and mop up. TOOOT."

## SEVEN

A large globular creature jellies in its seat. A unique animal that thrives off a duplex diet of junk food and sadistic opprobrium. It unleashes one of its fiendish schemes and Cubby watches humiliation roll toward him in a slow ugly wave. The options for escape are few—go to the bathroom, get sent to the principal, skip, start drugs, drop out. The probability exceeds chance that "Math Day" in the 3rd grade will leave the pupils feeling their filmy eyeballs cleft along the seams by a razor-thin blade.

"Brenda, go to the chalk board. Stand up straighter young lady. Now with the chalk..."

The other students, Teacher's unwitting agents, understand the condescension meant to impugn the girl's character and imply she doesn't possess the motor skills or know-how to wield chalk.

"Write the problem. Eleven times four."

This teacher's pedagogical style drags students through the motions assuming they will absorb the concepts by muscle memory. Remote control. Complete control. Multiplication by aggravation. Each child figures his or her problem and each wrong answer is forever crowned by acidulous laughter.

"Wrong again. What's wrong with you kids?"

"Maybe we don't eat the right breakfast cereal."

Teacher pulls a hard grimace from his arsenal.

"Thank you for volunteering to go next Mr. Zazuzay."

Danny A and Jimmy B laugh every time the teacher says "Zazuzay."

Cubby liked math until the teacher wrote, "Math is not Mr. Zazuzay's best subject" on the last report card. Now he wasn't so sure. His chin drops with dread as he trudges to the board and picks up the chalk. He looks back for instruction. A malicious grin consumes Teacher's face—the smile strung end to end would measure about twenty-eight feet, as it spans greasy lips, circles back over broad expanses of cheek, crisscrosses an ocean of jowl and mingles with the matrix of furrows that slope down from a meaty forehead.

"Seventeen times nine, Mr. Zazuzay."

Cubby feels sick. Some of the children GIGGLE, others TITTER. He doesn't know the answer, shrugs, looks to the class for help. His rivals anticipate failure. The teacher manipulates him like a marionette. Cubby closes his eyes and thinks about his parents. His mom would say, "Do the best you can, Honey." His dad would say, "Don't worry, school's a sham."

Cubby's mathematical mind goes blank. The numbers he copied on the board jump about and dance. A fox cornered by hounds—a hunter rolls up slow in a golf cart to finish him. Cubby can see Teacher getting ready to speak. The vibrations of pre-speech move through the tabs of flesh on his arms and jiggle toward the larynx.

"Hurry up Mr. Zazuzay. Don't waste my time."

Cubby turns to the board and writes, 1-5-3.

"That's wrong again. Why must you children guess when you don't know the answer? If one cannot speak, be silent. Say, *'I DON'T KNOW.'*"

Steel skewers drive into Cubby from obscure angles—through the rib cage to the heart, into the vertebra through the back of the neck, through the spine up into the brain.

"Cubby, can you hear me? Sit down."

The little boy has been robbed of the will to control his own movements.

"Move one leg at a time, let one foot fall after another, right, left, okay about-face, bend at the knees, sit."

Cubby puts his head down on the desk. His tear dikes swell. He doesn't want the class to see. He doesn't want Teacher to see. He struggles to hold it in.

Unobserved, Yadira Yaz, daughter of Mort's best friend Jimenez, works out the problem underneath her desk with a pocket calculator.

Since Teacher never gets up from his desk, a complex underground world has developed. The children pass comic books, notes, candies and black-market sundries around the room with clandestine stealth. Yadira smiles.

The children keep the top halves of their bodies immobile while the bottom halves gyrate in the free underground.

Yadira passes the calculator to Spencer, who works the problem on the board, smiles and passes it to Juan Sarto. Cubby receives a tap on the shoulder.

He doesn't look up. He's been fastened to the village stocks before. The kid next to him makes a PSSSS sound.

Cubby peeps one pale blue eye up and Cleophus Penny passes the calculator.

"Okay class, take out your spelling papers. If you can't do math, maybe your tiny minds can spell this week's very simple vocabulary words."

The children, skilled at doing two things at once, shuffle in the desks for their spelling papers without taking their eyes off of Cubby.

He punches in 17, hits the multiplication (X) sign, pushes the 9 and follows with the equal sign (=).

"One-fifty-three."

The shuffle of the spelling papers falls silent.

"Did you say something Mr. Zazuzay?"

Cubby's mind reels like the disk drive in a computer. He can't show Teacher the calculator, that would be suicide. Like the day Broderick Penny, Cleo's twin, dropped Mark A's candy bar. Teacher sucked it up like a vacuum, devouring the whole bar in front of the class. When Broderick got back from detention the class shunned him. Even his brother wouldn't talk to him at school. He had put "La Résistance" in jeopardy. Viva la résistance.

"I was wondering if, before we went on to spelling, if you could show us how to work out the problem."

The problem was still on the board.

The 28-foot smile appears. Teacher is always ready to seize a chance to demonstrate his superiority.

"It's very simple. First, you multiply the nine times seven. That's sixty-three. You carry the six, nine times one is nine, plus six is fiftee--"

He doesn't finish. He realizes that far ahead that Cubby's correct answer is still up on the board. The kids inhale triumph from the air. The occasional unfathomable victory is all they hope for. Cubby feels good. Like a cloud in trousers. He will not cry today. Today he will smile. And nobody, not even Teacher, can discount his happiness.

## EIGHT

Most of the customers at the hospital coffee bar wait patiently, in long lines, because they need a lift that coffee, a cookie or muffin might provide. Some are addicts who want to keep the needle out of the red, some are sleepwalkers fettering adenosine's death march, some offer themselves a reward because no one else will. And since the coffee bar is in a hospital some blot out grief, after a night sitting death watch, with a shot of dopamine. Kill time or kill pain. Her boss advised Angora on the first day not to ask, "How are you doing?" since the answers were often too much to carry home.

The rude fraction of customers is small but sticky. Mr. Jaguar may or may not return, but unhappy or entitled patrons are bound to cause a scene or act out at intervals. The spectrum ranges from the hungry or tired child's tantrum to the stressed-out driver's road rage to the disgruntled employee "going postal" with an automatic weapon to end the lives of people who worked by his side for years.

Each worker at the coffee bar has her own way of coping.

Renata has a knack for sincere apology. Customers believe her when she claims to be sorry she gave them whole milk instead of skim. Her boss, the owner of the coffee bar, doesn't like it when she appeases the very rudest with a bribe.

> "Your kindness is killing me. Comped muffins and free re-fills cut into the bottom line. Most of the customers won't be back until they need a wart removed from their ass or a colonoscopy, so it doesn't pay to be too nice."

Angora has already forgotten about Mr. Jaguar. She likes to go home and tell Mort about her day and move on. She doesn't dwell. She closes her eyes and breathes and forgets. On bad days, she might cry in the car before she drives home, which usually leaves her cleansed. If that doesn't work, there's always a glass of cheap red wine on the couch.

At 10am, a horde of regular customers on their 15-minute-break rush out of the elevator. Angora is ready, so the line moves quickly. The doctor looks at his watch. He doesn't have to be anywhere for five minutes. The secretary inhales a breath from her mocha. She doesn't know what to do with this gift moment. One customer throws a dollar tip—a buck and another buck until dead presidents fill the jar.

"The usual?"

"Yes! It's been crazy today."

"Thanks Angora, Sugar, you put the coffee in my coffee break."

"Thank you. Thank you. How was your daughter's birthday…"

The rush of leisure is like a hot bath after digging post holes for a fence in the sun, like a back massage after hauling sacks of cement, like a cold beer after delivering the mail up and down a hillside route in the rain. It's like a cool rain on your face after shoveling coal into the boiler of a cruise ship. It's like the initial in-breath of espresso crema after a mind-numbing morning on the phone. Moreover, it is the first jolt proffered by that espresso after a mind-numbing ass kissing week in a sidewalk café of Paris. The coffee's gallop through the veins is a springtime adventure to where the birds sing. Far from the usual elevator ride to the gallows, this return to the office becomes a slow jaunt to the art deco bordello for an afternoon of erotic indulgence. A cup of coffee is all the sunshine you'll get here.

Half the workers forsake the elevator and walk three flights of stairs. Their cordoned hearts pump caffeine and oxygen to the brain. Freedom rings!

Nix Graves, a boy of sixteen, Angora's new coworker, notices the change in atmosphere from behind the counter. Even though he considers this a dead-end job, so far he finds it "pretty kickback". Angora likes him but wishes he wouldn't squeeze his zits.

His peroxide hair has been dyed blue with Kool-Aid and anyone can see he fancies himself a punk rocker. The studded belt hangs around his waist. He prefers to spend time alone writing dark goth love poems and drawing pictures of executions. His favorite band is Black Flag. He saw their last show with Henry Rollins when he was seven years old. He'd read what he could about Rollins in zines, spent hours over pictures of the singer's tattoos and even listened to one of his spoken word albums. Nix's older brother, notorious in the local scene for an overdose on Jack Daniels, which people said he drank through a needle in his arm, left him a stack of the band's early records.

*It's not my imagination, I got a gun at my back…*

When Nix was twelve he gave himself a tattoo of the band's logo ▮▮▮▮ which has already faded with time. Nix finished his **GED** and wants to leave home, hence the job. Angora shows him how to pull shots and make the basic drinks—espresso, latte, cappuccino… He seems quiet, introspective. He hasn't said four extraneous words, but isn't shy.

He seems to have more than a bit of the misanthrope about him, the kind of kid who becomes susceptible to fringe anti-government militias of the right or left. He doesn't consider himself racist since he hates whites and blacks alike. He likes that Angora doesn't talk down to him. That she treats him like an equal. She can see behind his mask, recognizes the disguise; he reminds her of a young Mort banging his head against the world.

After a run of iced Americanos, Angora asks Nix to fill the ice. On the way, he pops into the bathroom and catches his reflection in the mirror showing a pus-filled whitehead on the tip of his nose.

"Being a teenager sucks."

He leans in and squeezes the head of the zit between his thumb and index finger which releases a blast of whitehead material that slaps the mirror like wet hamburger. Then he feels a presence. A man in a tan suit waits to wash his hands. He must have been in the stall. Nix steps up to the urinal, shields his cock from the man's vantage.

Consequently, a little pee dribbles onto his black jeans. Fuck. Nix's zipper roars up, strangely amplified by the acoustics.

He finds the ice machine out in an alcove off the hall without much effort. He finds a bucket, slides open the door. Cold air moves over his face and skin. The scoop is on top of the machine, but he puts his bare hands into the ice and pushes a large armful into the bucket. A dozen cubes miss the mark and skid in every direction across the floor.

At the espresso bar, the café manager helps Angora make coffee. A cup sells for three dollars even though the beans, heated water and labor cost pennies. American consumers will pay any price for convenience. The man in the tan suit orders a creme de menthe latte which Angora rings up on the cash register.

"I was in the rest room and one of your workers urinated," the man in the tan suit says to the manager.

"Yes sir."

"Well, he didn't wash his hands. That's unsanitary."

Nix appears with the bucket of ice. His hands turned blue after he ran his fingers through his hair. The man in the tan suit doesn't mention the whitehead material hitting the mirror or the splash of urine.

Nix's presence silences him. The kid stands six foot-one in steel-toed boots.

"I'm sorry. I'll have a talk with him about it, he's new."

The man in the tan suit puts a nickel and three pennies in the tip jar.

He sips his coffee a bit too early. "Owwww!"

"Nix. This man says you didn't wash your hands after you used the bathroom."

Nix pictures a slow-motion collision between a black boot and the groin area of tan suit pants.

"It's important to wash up for health reasons. People can get really sick. Have you heard of (she whispers) e-Coli?"

Nix can't be bothered to feign embarrassment.

"I have to deliver a blueberry scone and a vanilla mocha to the doctor's office across the street, you two watch the shop."

The manager walks away and thinks about which movie to rent with her girlfriend at Blockbuster. I wonder if she's seen *Natural Born Killers*. I love Juliette Lewis.

Angora reaches into the pocket of her apron and voilà—Snickers bar. She offers half to her new coworker. The man's complaint and the manager's reproach made him feel the way he did around his parents. Like the time his dad threw a chair and the brother got a knife from the kitchen and the father stood stone-faced when he realized his misfit child could in fact slit his throat. Nix will never forget the cold way his father said, "Get out of my house" or the cool way his brother turned and walked out the door without looking back.

Nix's brother said he would hole up in a squat on the far side of town and promised to visit. He seemed different when he came, lost. Nix heard his brother was selling speed, sniffing glue, and even at eleven years old he knew his older brother (and first idol before Henry Rollins) would never come home, not really.

## NINE

Mort cruises down the freeway in the '64 Cadillac hearse, peering occasionally at the directions which lie on the passenger side of the bench seat. One of his favorite driving songs, cranked up really high, blares through the speakers and Gabby Gaborno sings:

> *The more I'd drive the more things got worse…Take me to that Cadillac hearse…Cadillac, Cadillac hearse…*

After a patron left the hearse to the museum in his will, PT restored the car to its original macabre glory. If it could wear stiletto heels and give wild blow jobs, Lilli joked that he'd move into the garage, even though she'd fallen as hard for the big, loose Caddy. Behind the wheel, with all that road going, she feels invincible. Mort painted hot rod flames on the front quarter panels and air brushed the museum's skull logo along the side and PT sewed curtains for the back using a pattern one of the oddball regulars swiped from a file cabinet at a mortuary.

Chaz, or "Chuckles" as everyone calls him, comes in every day before his job as an embalmer's assistant, a boon for the museum, since he has donated several items of antique funeral equipment—a bone saw, a siphon and a tin of dried-up facial reconstruction putty found in a dank storage closet. He spent his first paycheck on an expensive suit and mirror sunglasses. After a month pumping fluid in and out of bodies, he seemed like a different person. Not ghoulish, per se,… but taken on vacated airs. Not only did he drink more than had been his habit, he'd discovered a taste for exotic cocktails. Having taken up a stool in the bar next to the museum, he spends evenings over a trilogy of chilled gins in upright glasses rinsed with absinthe and dosed with a French aperitif and orange liqueur. People he'd known from the block hardly recognized him.

Driving toward his appointment, Mort thinks about suicide. How different the world, if each member of his generation—Gen X—participated in a mass exodus. X as in missing from the equation. "Live Fast, Die Young" was the motto—struck as a pose or accepted as fate. He can see the crowd in Times Square waiting for the ball to drop on the millennium like a guillotine.

The media could call it 'Y2K - X.'

Kurt Cobain showed the way.

In the end, when the moment comes to swallow the cyanide how many will hold back? The previous generations still believed in self-preservation and Hallmark cards. Jim Stark in *Rebel Without a Cause* didn't go over the edge; James Dean corrected the writer's mistake. The "blank generation" loves a spectacle. They would "chicken" from a desire to witness the crime. Imagine the sublime aftermath of sixty-five million beautiful corpses! Surf the pandemonium. Be the one… who lived, however ignominiously, to tell the story. The grand golden parachute opens on this insignificant cavalcade—the millennials can bury us and fill our pointless slacker jobs. Shut up Little Big Man.

There isn't much traffic outside of rush hour, since most commuters spend their days rotting behind a desk in some office. Mort takes the exit and pushes the hearse up to the stop sign. The tape in the cassette deck flips mechanically to the other side.

Mort had dubbed the mixtape *Soundtrack for a Death Museum* for PT and Lilli his first day on the job. Jello Biafra of Dead Kennedys sings:

> *Tonight's the night that we ride the truck, going downtown gonna beat up drunks, your turn to drive, I'll bring the beer…*

Mort presses the accelerator and the big engine opens up—man, she is good on curves. The client's street appears, so Mort cuts the wheel sharp and the tires screech. The killer machine screams and hollers and races the engine up the block sounding like an invasion against the quietus of the tree-lined street. A boy peeks from behind the blinds in one of the windows. The sunlight filters down through the leafless branches of jacaranda and gold medallion. The houses seem freshly painted, the lawns made verdant by automated sprinklers.

The hearse roars up the block rubber on asphalt, the tires turn madly, only to brake in front of a midsize house with a picket fence. The pickets are covered with patchy black mildew. Someone should mow the lawn; the weeds have grown waist high. Mort counts seven shades of green in the yard. A light juice green ivy consumes the front of the house like the natural world wants to swallow it whole. Mort remains in the hearse. He checks the address and lets the song finish.

He secures The Club to the steering wheel, hits the kill switch behind the seat and steps out of the car. He locks the door, shuts it, pulls the handle to check. He pushes the alarm. BEEP BOOP.

The air is cooler here than downtown. A chill runs Mort's bones through his skin. He gathers composure and walks through the gate. Boots disturb brittle leaves. On the third step, a snail explodes. The vacuous creature spreads like a pasty egg yolk with bits of shell in the mix. The circle between life and death plays out under the carpet of leaves. A troop of red ants has already been dispatched to cart away what they can use.

Mort steps more carefully. He doesn't want to cause further harm. Inside, a frail man, alerted by the screech of tires, peers from behind ashen curtains. The skull logo on the hearse matches the ad in the telephone book where he found the museum's number.

Mort raps five times in rapid succession on the brass escutcheon before the old man opens the door. He looks into the house and feels dizzy. Overstimulated. The history of the world in objects seems to be piled flotsam from floor to ceiling. Candlesticks and pipes of wine and books and electronic equipment—reel to reel tapes, amplifiers, equalizers, a victrola—a suit of armor, a collection of knives, a mannequin head, one very small suitcase in gray-color cloth, a full-sized elk stuffed with sawdust, a box with a thousand spoons, another with a thousand forks. Spanners and coils of rope. Shapes and colors and textures.

This guy's got some kind of obsessive-compulsive pack rat disorder.

The old man is much like Mort pictured him over the phone—short, perhaps shrunken with age, a shock of hair like steel wool that hasn't been combed. His ears are long. His gray eyes are magnified by thick glasses balanced on an old potato nose.

Mort is much like the old man pictured him. Youthful, angry, misunderstood. Possibly some kind of skinhead, but also looking like he's come from chemotherapy.

"Come in young man. Sit down."

Mort settles into the divan.

"The suspension in that old couch gave up the ghost long ago. We have a lot in common that way."

As the old man fades into reverie, he dips in to the gallery of scoundrels who lingered through the wee hours in the warm sound bath of Miles Davis's trumpet and on to the small coterie of ladies wooed prone by Sinatra's wistful lullabies and uncountable bottles of cheap red wine, spilled in droplets or by the glass, with each stain a Rorschach of memory.

Mort sits with the patience of an unemployed man.

A grimace takes over the old man's face and gives it a violent shake. An electric bolt of pain hit like a policeman's nightstick.

"This way to the gas…"

He releases a stinging flatulence that fills the room. The grimace reminds Mort of Angora at the hospital giving birth. He expects the bloody head of an infant to pop out of the old man's asshole.

"Was there something you meant to ask?"

"Um, perhaps we should start with your name. TOOOT."

Mort reaches in his pocket for the notebook.

"You should have a questionnaire for life's stupid details."

Mort jots this down in a little box at the top corner of his notepad.

"My name is Leif Negdin."

Mort scrawls the name. He should have verified the spelling since it would be essential to get it correct on the note. He figures he can get the name off of the check, then again, it might be smarter to get cash, since some people kill themselves for financial reasons.

Negdin's first name, at least, sounds Scandinavian. Mort's own great-grandfather emigrated from Norway in the 1880s.

"A good suicide note always considers its reader. Who will you leave behind? TOOOT."

"I uh, mmm, have a few relatives in the east. They should see it, I suppose, no. No children, no wife, no one close. A cousin…"

Mort wants to ask about friends. Instead, he smiles revealing his broken grin and traces over the notes.

"My cronies are either dead or dead to me."

Mr. Negdin's gray eyes fixate on something Mort can't see. The past maybe. Mort scans the room and touches the objects with his eyes. Each one has a story about to be lost forever. The suicide note could be an encyclopedia. Someday school children might copy their own final missives from Negdin. Most will steal the best lines verbatim.

"Is the suicide note for the relatives or did you intend a more global epitaph? TOOOT."

Mort senses the question-and-answer interview isn't working.

"No, wait. This is awkward. Why don't you tell me why you want to leave a note and what you need me to help with. TOOOT."

"I knew you were a greenhorn. Have courage."

Mort stands up and whistles a tune from Billie Holiday through his broken tooth.

"Ha ha ha. I saw Billie Holiday at the Down Beat, maybe '49 or '50."

"Wow! TOOOT."

"Her eyes were black with black embers alive behind the pupils. She looked so tired, but yanked out the most doleful shade of blue. If you could paint with her blues… If you could mix them up and slap them on a canvas, you could bring the beholder to his knees. I guess I was what you'd call a Beatnik, ha, though we didn't call ourselves that."

Negdin's eyelids shut like a roll top desk.

"What did you call yourselves? TOOOT."

"Serious."

Negdin's voice croaks like a frog in a dry wash.

"I feel pulled apart, my boy. On one side this pain in my joints drives like a horse to the barn. Or to the grave. Brief is man's life on earth, Yada Yada. It's no place for the old. Some people die too late. Ya. On the other side is the desire to watch one more poppy explode into bloom and pet one more cat."

"I noticed you don't have a tv. TOOOT."

"So?"

"People say 'Yada' on tv. TOOOT."

"That lazy language is in the air, even a recluse can't avoid it. You can't hide from it in books or music or art. *The Honeymooners* killed television for me. Stupidest thing I ever saw. People pulled up chairs to sit in front of the tv. Ha! When you look at paintings in a gallery, you stand up. Sit in a bar, sit behind a desk. It's the same. I got out early, but you can't avoid it. I don't tell people what to do with their lives. I tried to do something with mine…"

This guy needs a memoir, rather than a fuckin' suicide note. The man could have slid the straight razor over his wrists. He didn't have to call the Death Museum. If he wants to die, it's his business. Why shouldn't any free citizen of his own private utopia do as he pleases with his body? A sound mind has nothing to do with it. If some old dude wants to shuffle off, the planet has billions of desperate people trolling thrift stores for a vintage Cardigan.

"Would you like coffee?"

"No thanks, I had my fix. TOOOT."

Mr. Negdin stands up slowly, a chore, rather than the simple motion most take for granted.

"Would you like me to show you around?"

"Yes. This place is like the Smithsonian. TOOOT."

"The Smithsonian is extraordinary."

"I've never been. TOOOT."

Mort follows Negdin down a narrow hallway.

"Why do people do that?"

"What? TOOOT."

"Compare things to experiences they've never had."

"Imagination, I guess."

"Hmmm. Here's the bathroom, if you need to take a shit."

There's a high tank toilet—water cached above and a pull chain to flush out the bowl. The seat is up, the bowl is stained yellowish-brown, like a rust brought on by stagnant urine. It smells of old piss.

Whitish-gray water sits low in the basin below the tap.

"I hope you don't mind the smell, I'm used to it myself, try to conserve water, you know."

"Same at our house."

Mort smiles revealing his broken grin. The tour guide moves slowly. Mort stands in front of a shut door, painted green with long rough brush strokes. It could be a closet, but Mort has a queer feeling about it.

Negdin reaches the bedroom. The twin bed in the center of the room has four sandalwood posts, Mort drags his fingers over the skulls carved into the bed knobs—this guy sculpted his own deathbed.

"I noticed your art collection, some of the abstracts are decent. TOOOT."

"Walter Benjamin, who killed himself with morphine rather than be delivered into the hands of Nazis, said that 'of all the ways of acquiring books, writing them oneself is regarded as the most praiseworthy method.' I feel the same about painting. When I was young I knew artists who'd give away their canvases for a bit of love or a square meal, but for the itinerant precarity of my life, eating morphine in my own way, I couldn't guarantee their preservation. I lived in the city of the dead. By the time I got back, I couldn't afford to buy the paintings I liked, so I took up the brush. In the end, I painted much less than most people who paint."

"I like these."

"They show some craft, but not an original canvas in the bunch."

"This black wedge in the ochre field is…agonal. TOOOT."

Mort lets the stack of canvases fall to rest and steps up to an oil painting mounted on the wall, aggressively like he wants to fight it.

"That's my grandfather. Torgi Negdinson. He was a sea captain. Quite the rake, if you'd believe the scuttlebutt. Some called him a pirate."

"A pirate? TOOOT."

"May or may not be a tall tale, but there were one-hundred-sixty-four acts of piracy on the high seas last year."

For a second, Negdin's voice sounds vital and rigorous before it falls into its filed rasp.

Mort sneers at the symbolism—the hourglass, the sextant. Alas poor Goya's staid skull on a shelf above to remind us how quiet is life at home. As he continues to look, an appreciation gets the better of him. It's the tension between the portrayed man's élan vital and the still life the painter trapped him in.

"His son, my father, was an inventor."

"What did he invent? TOOOT."

"Nothing useful. That turned out to be a problem between him and mother. 'Tom the tinker in his workshop,' she called him."

Mort looks at the photographs on the bureau for a clue to Negdin's personal history. Was he a widower? There had to be someone close at one point. A snapshot on the night table catches his eye, a man stands before a public monument, posed on vacation perhaps. The rugged, bearded man smiles. On closer inspection, he seems familiar. On the back, "Love Papa 6/61."

"Young man, are you with me?"

"Yes. I got caught by this photo, is it your father? TOOOT."

Mort meets Negdin in the hallway, a smirk of reminiscence on his face.

"A friend. He had a paternal air, acted like everyone's father. He passed a long time ago."

"Time slaughters all. TOOOT."

"I'm sorry, but that toot is quite bothersome. Have you been afflicted with it long?"

"I've had it for years, don't notice it any more. Like that smell in your bathroom. TOOOT."

"Would you mind if I tried something?"

He follows Negdin down another hall, through a door the color of morning glories and into a room Mort designates the library. There are shelves of books on every wall. The room is dusty and both men's sinuses clench. The nose hairs catch some of the dust, the sinuses catch more, but enough slips into the lungs to labor the breath.

Aside from books—Rilke's *Letters to Cézanne*, Apollinaire's treatise on Cubism, poems by Frank O'Hara, missives by Breton and Creval—there are hundreds of comics from the 20s to the 40s. A desk covered with folios, files, scrolls, personal papers and drawings idles in one corner. The floor space in between is taken up by boxes, packed full.

"I gave up organizing this shit."

The interview feels like it's on a smoother tack. The house has helped Mort see more of the man than his words.

Negdin dives into one box after another. He mumbles various letters of the alphabet as he piles through the junk and Mort puts A through F together. Each box contains items that start with the same letter.

Box #1: ashtray, abacus, ascot…ax.

"My father has an invention that might prevent that annoying whistle."

Mort wants to confess a love for his affliction. It gives him leave to reflect on where it came from and serves as a metaphor for his new priorities.

Box #2: bag, beret, bleach bottle, bodkin, brick…

As the man digs through box after box, Mort rethinks his position on the sanity clause. Perhaps crazy people can't be held responsible for their own lives and shouldn't be allowed to end them.

"I can't seem to remember what he called the damn thing. But I'm sure it will solve your whistle problem."

Negdin rummages a box that contains bent metal pipes, playing cards, part of a pitch fork, a pussy willow (dried), a python (rubber), a thousand old pens borrowed from donut shops across the country and hundreds of photographs.

One of the pictures, which could be of a young Negdin with Ray Johnson and Anni Albers at Black Mountain College, gets shuffled under before Mort can get a look at it.

Mort moves so he can see over Negdin's shoulder as the man comes upon a stack of pornographic magazines.

"It's not a pacifier."

Negdin abandons "P" and takes up the search in the next box. Mort kneels and thumbs through the porno mags. A man sits on a large boulder, which—*No, it can't be, can it?*—turns out to be his own nut sac snowballed by elephantiasis. He turns the page and another man helps lift his friend's gargantuan balls up into a thatched hut.

"This guy's balls look like a Hoppity Hop."

"My father called this a 'Paper Winder.' It needs a battery. Here's one."

Negdin holds a curious device up to a roll of toilet paper. He pulls the trigger and it extracts the paper from its roll lightning quick and stores it inside the machine."

"Huh, I could use that. TOOOT."

A fantasy about the trouble he could cause in the fast-food industry imposes itself. He could steal all of the toilet paper. Mort grips onto the couch arm to pull himself back into the world.

"Ah here it is!"

Negdin drops the Paper Winder and dives back into the box to disinter some sort of mouthpiece.

"Here, put this in your mouth."

Mort sets down the magazine and takes the little contraption from his client. He blows some dust off, examines and shines it like an apple against his shirt.

"Give it a try."

Mort slides the thing into his mouth. It tastes like old shoe leather, but fits like a glove over his teeth. He thought it would do more to obscure speech, but as he rotates his jaw around, it feels okay.

"Drink to me, drink to my health."

Negdin brightens at the success, his wrinkles take on a gray glow.

"One of my father's designs. I forget what he called it. It was in the "S" box. He tried to market it to people who talked with a lisp. Never manufactured. That's the proto-type."

"That's really…Wow, I can't believe it. TOOOT."

"You can keep it. Please."

Negdin looks tired again. He backs up to a stuffed chair, plops down and raises a pall of dust, the particles redistribute themselves around the room. Mort slips the "S-Device" back into his mouth.

"Thanks a lot, sir. That's kind of you."

Mort starts to doubt his former position on suicide. Perhaps Negdin needs company in the lonesome latter years of his life. Some way to tell the stories of these treasures one more time.

The magazine in Mort's hand falls open on *The Inventions of Professor Lucifer G. Butts* by Rube Goldberg. He thinks of Mouse Trap, of Cubby, of Angora. Wow. The specter of money follows on her heels into his thoughts. He needs to get paid. This poor old man's demise is tied with a 13-knot noose to the future of his family.

"This stuff is incredible. I wonder though, you didn't have kids, any regrets?"

"Mmmm, no. Hmm, yes, well, we haven't talked about money yet. I can spend two hundred on this operation in toto."

"Two hundred will be fine."

## TEN

Angora stares out at the skyline. She presses a photograph into a family album. A signal from one part of her brain indicates that her elbow feels pain against the hard wood of the dinner table. A half glass of purple merlot resides in the grip of one hand.

The usual array of yellow and white lights on the downtown buildings are festooned with red and green for the season. The tallest visible building, a bank, sports seven strings of light meant to represent a Xmas tree.

Half of the photographs were from Halloween—Mort dressed as the Stinky Cheese Man and Angora as a blonde Marilyn Monroe in the wig, white halter dress and slingback pumps. Cubby has always loved to dress up; the photo in her hand shows him as a ninja on roller skates. Angora helped Cubby eat the mini chocolate bars he collected trick-or-treating around the neighborhood and now the bulging pillow case in the photo is nearly empty. A few Life Savers and other hard candies he doesn't care for remain. The pictures from Thanksgiving were overexposed as the film got jammed in their Instamatic camera. They would have shown Angora and her mother with the turkey and a pumpkin pie fresh from the oven. One photo would have shown the boys with hands on their bellies after stuffing the cornucopia into their mouths like ravenous animals.

Cubby sleeps, pillow cast aside, his face coalesces with a stuffed Eeyore. A blanket and Speed Racer comforter pulled up tight are tuck and rolled under his chin.

Mort walks in with a bouquet of flowers—a spray of pink mums, baby's breath and dried white roses. He notes the half-empty wine bottle, walks straight past her to the bedroom. The dirty nail of his index finger traces along the wall calendar and stops on a little red letter P.

"P for period."

He walks back to the aluminum room, hands Angora the flowers, opens the front door and exits where he just came in.

"I'll be right back, Honey."

As soon as he clears the front walk, he breaks into a run. Through the window, Angora watches him sprint across the street and disappear around the corner. She sips her wine from a small glass—kills it in a gulp. She puts the flowers in an old jelly jar with some water. The ebb tide of hormones feels like the ocean sucking out before a tsunami. Her thoughts churn in the mill stone of her brain and grind down to tiny angry bits.

Mort had always wanted to amplify and record her monthly endometrial demolition. He liked to tease her that it would be the most excruciating record since *Metal Machine Music*. Banned in every country. Riots would break out in its wake. Men would cower as the women ripped it all to shreds. The favorite chair unseamed from its back to its farting place, the remote dashed against the wall, the porn set ablaze, the beer guzzled, the Sunday project taken from the garage on a wreckful joyride, the suits slashed, the LPs left in the sun to warp… The urge to destroy is natural and contagious. The cry of the eagle, the ride of the Valkyrie and the hunt of the Maenads broil inside her with the scream of the banshee. Faster, pussycat! Kill! Kill!

Angora watches Mort dash across the street. A Buick Skylark, green in the yellow street light, skids to a halt in front of him. The driver shakes a fist and Mort's lips mouth the words, *"Fuck You!"*

"I wonder if he made that pathetic tooting sound."

A second later, her husband bursts through the door, a Snickers bar in one hand, leaning forward he draws breath to relieve the stitch in his side. Such romantic gestures should have a positive effect on her mood, he risked his life and all, but chocolate can't solve every problem.

"Nice try, but where have you been?"

"I -huh huh huh I huh got a job."

Mort, in a desperate move, slaps the entire two-hundred-dollar wad on the table. He reminds himself to keep his mouth shut. He silently repeats the word "listen" three times. He forces a smile and reveals his new mouthpiece.

"You also have a job here. You have a son or have you forgotten?"

"I know."

"You want Cubby to drop out of school? He says he won't go back. What are you going to do?"

"What are you talking about?"

"His teacher…"

"What did the teacher do now?"

"He humiliates Cubby every day. He makes Cubby feel stupid and the other kids pick on him."

Angora's eyelashes are wet. Mort puts his arms out and sucks her into an embrace. The body heat feels pleasant. It's been a long time since he's been able to provide comfort. He usually digs his own grave, says something to undermine it, to flame the situation and piss her off.

His day of work has restored some confidence. The gray cloud of neurasthenic ennui eases—exposing clear, blue thoughts. Meanwhile, a steady stream of doubt and fear roll through the factory of Angora's mind on a conveyor belt as her homunculus assembles some infernal commodity.

"Did you talk to the teacher?"

"No! I don't want to talk to the teacher, he scares the shit out of me. You need to talk to him."

"I'll go to the school tomorrow."

"What's this job?"

"I started a business."

"A business? Ha. You said you got a job."

"It's gonna be big."

"We need money now, Mort. We need to move Cubby to a new school. We need health insurance."

"This is money. Wait, move? We can't move. I need time to develop this."

"You had time. You haven't worked in a year."

He follows her back toward the bedroom.

"January. Mort loses job. February, March, April, May… July. No job. August no job. September, still no job."

She flips the calendar until December and chucks it across the room. It dies like a shot bird and falls behind the bed.

"I went out to look for a job. I went down to the Death Museum."

"The Death Museum!"

"Let me finish. This old man called and wanted to kill himself and he needed a suicide note. He paid me to write it and take care of a few details."

Angora lets out a deep, systemic groan loaded with a dull drowsy grief. A fuse in her brain sizzles as synaptic connections blow. Her legs crumple and she folds in a mess to the floor. Her limbs thrash spasmodically on the carpet. Gutter curses spill from her mouth, a consortium of "fuck" "shit" "dick" "ass" and other bodily oaths and curses from languages she doesn't even know. The drum of her balled-up fists intensifies. Mort wants to tear out his own blue eyes. This is his fault.

He puts his hand on her shoulder, a mistake. Her sights lock on and she slaps wildly.

"Angora, this is real. I can make this work. I can make money."

"Aagghhhh!" she screams—unable to form words.

*Why me? Why me? Why me?* repeats over and over in her mind, but at such a high speed it feels like electric gibberish. It whips around her brain like a bullet ricocheting off the walls of her skull. Wild! She's legally insane.

"Whymewhymewhyme!"

He strokes her Cosmopolitan hair and the phrase moves slower, "Why me? Why me? Why me?" He secures one arm around her neck and puts the other underneath her thighs. He lifts with his legs and picks her up. She feels heavier than when they first dated. He carries her to the bedroom and lays her out on the mattress like a pressed shirt you might wear to a funeral. He pulls a blanket over. He digs into her calves which feel like knotted wood. She looks so tired. He gets the trash can from the bathroom, puts in a new bin liner in case she has to puke. He puts a glass of water on the nightstand.

Cubby slumbers peacefully holding Eeyore close. His legs hang off the bed. Mort scoots him over, tucks the blanket in, stretches to kiss his son on the forehead.

He collapses in the green chair.

Tomorrow. Tomorrow.

ELEVEN

Mort sits in the green rocking chair and trips on his exhaustion like a drug. He imagines, in the way Maxine Hong Kingston and Allen Ginsberg tried to psychically levitate the Pentagon in 1973, that he could, somehow with his mind, put out the lights around the city. He'd like to see the stars better and to watch people come outside and meet their neighbors for the first time. Sleep beckons as eyes grow heavy. He readjusts the cushion and finds the blonde wig Angora had worn on Halloween. As he falls Lethe-wards, his notepad slips between the cushion. Steam rises out of a tea cup and carries hints of Earl Grey and mint. The warm mug in his palm feels like a removed organ.

The phone RINGS. Clock says, 3:33am. It RINGS again, loud against the previous dead silence. The answering machine picks up on the third RING and plays a riff from The Clash.

*...face the new religion, Everybody's sittin' 'round watchin' television...*

Mort's voice follows, "Leave a message." BEEP.

"If you're there, pick up. Come on Mort, I'm in the fucking jail, ese. Hello?"

Mort smiles revealing his mouthpiece to no one. He should change the message on the machine. Jimenez is a good friend, but a terrible joker. He'd used this line before.

"Qué pasa, Jefe?"

"I'm in jail, that's what!"

"It's 3-in-the-morning dude, no jokes."

"This ain't no joke, Sport. I'm not even sure where... I was out of it when they brought me in. They took my snakeskin belt and my shoelaces. The screws said they gonna ship me to maximum security. They took my fucking shoelaces. No room at the inn, homey. I need that lawyer friend of yours, call my editor at La Revuelta, tell her why I'm gonna miss the deadline, and go down to CPS and pick up Yadira."

"Slow down, slow down. Where's Silvia?"

"It's a long story, Man, they gonna deport her or some shit, get Yadira and a lawyer."

The pen on his lap bounces on the floor; he pulls on a dirty shirt and the same paint-speckled pants. He pulls on the mismatched socks and laces up his Dr. Marten boots. He finds his wallet and the car keys.

What did his best friend say? Child Protective Services? Jail? Deportation?

He turns circles. Makes coffee and grabs his checkbook. He remembers the rent is due, visualizes the money in their account. Not enough to bail anyone out.

Cubby's head is still pressed against Eeyore. Mort listens to the soft breath. It's the best sound in the world. Angora snores with her mouth open like a well. Her tongue looks dry. Mort runs a hand over his shaved head.

If a fire starts, she'll never wake up. He nudges her. She moans, but doesn't rouse from sleep.

"Angora, Angora."

He shakes harder.

"Uhhh."

"I have to go out, Jimenez is in jail. I have to pick up Yadira."

Angora doesn't open her burnt sienna eyes. Her head throbs. She might vomit.

"Angora, I have to go. Wake up."

Angora pulls the pillow over her head. Mort stomps out. He steps into the dark of the little boy's bedroom, pulls back the covers and lifts him up.

"You said I could have my own motorcycle."

"It's okay, go back to sleep." The mouthpiece Mr. Negdin had given Mort, the S-Device, slips out onto the floor and gets lost in the darkness under Cubby's bed.

"Shit. TOOOT."

Cubby's gotten heavier. Mort reflects on the way his son's legs just keep going and remembers how baby Cubby fit wrist to elbow. As he plops the boy down on the bed with his mom, he feels a twinge in his lower back.

Mort turns a circle.

He pulls a chair out of the kitchen, which bangs on the bedroom door and leaves a bright blue scratch. He presses the test button on the smoke detector. Nothing. He fishes a 9-volt battery out of the junk drawer, extracts the old battery and replaces it. The chair wobbles but doesn't fail. Mort looks down on his family in the bed. Cubby snuggles tight to his mother.

Mort presses the test button, BEEEEP!

Angora groans.

In the next minute, Mort is in the beat-up Toyota on his way to Child Protective Services. No traffic. A red light signals him to stop. He taps his fingers on the wheel and waits for the green. What the fuck is this 8-track player? And Del Shannon? The intense red glare causes him to squint. No one is around. He doesn't push play. The signal doesn't seem to know he's there or mocks him intentionally. Mort puts the beat-up Toyota in reverse. He rolls back and forward to trigger the sensor for the signal.

He looks around inside the car.

"We'll have to get some more 8-tracks."

He wants to run the light. He pictures Yadira, her long black hair uncombed, curled up on a cot, scared to death. His foot lifts off the brake. The beat-up Toyota inches forward. A black and white squad car turns onto the perpendicular street. Mort's shoe depresses the accelerator. The cop car approaches. Mort slams his foot to the brake. The light is still red, as the Toyota jerks to a stop, the nose inches past the limit line. The light on the perpendicular street finally changes from green to yellow.

As the police cruiser rolls up, the light goes red. Mort's signal flashes green and he hits the gas. The cop doesn't slow down and rolls through the red light into the intersection and Mort has to slam the brake as the cruiser passes. The cop keeps going. The beat-up Toyota idles in the middle of the street. The odometer reads, 88,887 miles (plus another 100,000 that had already rolled over.) Mort pounds the wheel. Not the years, the mileage. The Toyota's windows are rolled up, so the world can't hear his cry for help.

•••

Jimenez Yaz cools in a cell with his head against the bar. It's too noisy to sleep. Footsteps halt outside and the guard bangs his nightstick against the bar where Jimenez's head rested. The knell reverberating through his bones shouldn't be confused with the Liberty Bell.

"You're gonna wish you never crossed the river, wetback."

•••

"I'm here to get Yadira Yaz. TOOOT."

Mort looks bedraggled. His body odor smells ripe, pungent and even self-repugnant. Like a cadaver. What the hell is up with my hormones?

"It says here the girl is a Mexican national. She's going to be deported. Her mother was already shipped out."

Mort is exasperated. The social worker stares into a computer. They've been through this three times. He explained how he and his wife were the girl's "godparents" except they were atheist and preferred to be called "godless parents." The guy couldn't get it. Some people passed through life reading a script.

"Her father sent me down here to pick her up. There's been a mistake. TOOOT."

"There's nothing I can do."

"Let me talk to your supervisor. TOOOT."

"Look man, come back in the morning. The girl's asleep. There's no one here can help you."

The blood pumps into Mort's hands. He looks down the length of his arm and is surprised by barred, white knuckles. The social worker's nose looks like a bomb site. He's already pushed the button to call security.

The uniformed guard behind Mort stands a foot shorter, but stocky with a thick neck. The guard braces himself and brandishes a can of Cap-stun.

"You can't expect us to hand kids over to anyone who asks."

Mort backs out of the CPS. He doesn't take his eyes off the guard or the social worker.

The two men monitor each slow step until Mort stumbles back out on the street and rubs the bristles on his shaved head.

"Another night, another psycho."

The social worker nods and picks up the remains of a baloney sandwich, washes it down with cold coffee from a Styrofoam cup.

Mort walks up to the pay phone on the corner. He rubs the stubble on his square jaw. The streets are silent, deserted. A light comes on in a house near the pay phone as a laborer wakes up to start his day. Mort thinks about the sound coffee makes when it gurgles up out of the percolator. He can smell it. The colors in the air remind him of Mark Rothko.

Mort takes some loose change from his pocket. George Washington's wig is comically archaic, representative of a country founded on fad and fast fashion.

There's no slot for a coin, a placard on the phone reads, "Calling cards only."

•••

Jail wasn't a new concept for Jimenez—he'd sucked Trouble's tit like she was his wet nurse since the days when he delivered weed through his neighborhood on a bike the way other kids delivered newspapers. When he was in second grade, he saw a picture of wheat on the side of a flour sack.

"Teacher, what is this?"

"That's wheat."

"My dad's got a lot of wheat. He says I'm gonna trim it up and sell it."

"No, no. Not weed. Wheat. W-H-E-A-T. You make bread with it."

"Dad says we'll be making lots of bread."

In high school, he was suspended after he stole a half dozen pink polo shirts and penny loafers from the football teams' locker room. He was caught after he made a bonfire on the quad. Jimenez got expelled after he exploded an M-80 his cousin smuggled in from TJ outside an ROTC drill. Some dude shit his dress blues when the shock wave shattered a window. When the instructor cut his hand while picking up the broken glass, he knew he was in deep.

An uncle in the Brown Berets helped him get into City College where he earned solid marks writing essays about Ché Guevara, Flores Magón and Oscar Zeta Acosta. Second semester, he got tossed out of college for boosting textbooks from the university store.

He had no regrets.

His most recent arrests have been more political. He was taken from a picket line with farm workers, busted at a demonstration against the War in the Gulf. He loved pranks and any stunt that tossed a monkey wrench into the machine. Through brash acts of civil disobedience Jimenez became a believer in direct action.

This rap was different. A cop lay in the street bowed low and bloodied with his mustache pressed against the asphalt. A chunk of skull removed, the hole black deep like the void behind Saturn in Goya, oozes brain and gray gore.

He remembered a yell, "Go back where you came from, wet-back!"

Racists are the dumbest people. His forefathers were Spanish priests. They were racist too! They beat his grandmother's people when they wouldn't plow the soil. Go back? His grandmother's people have been here 13,000 years. Shit. He was born at Chula Vista Community hospital. Yo, Magónismo!

He supposed, in the time given for reflection in the cell, that this attack was related to an exposé he'd written for La Revuelta on the mayor's office. He'd dug up some minor mismanagement of funds, a trifle any adept politician could brush aside with double speak and denial, nothing that would get a man killed like journalists in Mexico risked every day.

As a guard's boot crashes into his balls, he thinks about his daughter and his girlfriend and offers to no one in particular a prayer for their safety. Though it surprises him, some, he doesn't consider it a renunciation of his lifelong and fraught atheism, rather, in the dim light of the cell it feels easy to call on a higher power for help. Maybe because it's easy, it isn't worth much. Abject people in churches around the world pray for salvation from the routine misery of their lives and have prayed for thousands of years without results—it isn't that desperation makes you believe in things that aren't real—but despair makes you look in the wrong direction. Instead of looking up you need to look in.

All the suffering in the world doesn't need to be lifted, just enough to let people squeak by. He worked to relieve some of that burden, but carrying more than his share, he wants help.

After this ordeal, I'll come out Superman. If I come out. What good was a character of steel when you're strapped to a table for lethal injection, you know?

The toe cap of a boot cracks a rib. His body absorbs the draconian punishment like a drum as the gang of police add their kicks to the throng.

THUD. CRACK. CRISP CRISP. BOMP.

"Silvia," he groans. "Yadi…"

Jimenez loses consciousness unaware his best friend is on the other side of a wall of bureaucratic red tape.

"My friend's name is Jimenez Yaz. Yaz. Y-A-Z. TOOOT."

"The computer doesn't show any Jimenez Yaz in custody here."

Mort gives up and calls his lawyer friend, who was a specialist in corporate law, but smart enough to fathom a next move.

"Go home, I'll see what I can do."

The morning traffic empties onto the freeway. It's 5am. The sun wasn't up but the eastern sky phased from black to gray in the nautical twilight.

He hadn't done any of the important tasks his friend begged him to do. He felt like a total failure. He leans back in the green chair and stares at the steel and glass buildings.

"Which one houses the city jail? Sorry, my friend. I could never make anything work right."

Angora appears from the bedroom. Her left hand presses her forehead with the same gesture her mother would use to check for a temperature. Her hair always seems under control.

"I thought I heard you. What's going on? I had to throw up and found Cubby next to me. I thought you bugged out."

Her shoulder brushes the wall, innards mixed up, as her gyroscope tilts with nausea. The anger was still there, in her mind, but her body felt drained of fight.

"Jimenez called from jail. He wanted me to pick up Yadira before she got deported, but CPS wouldn't let me have her. So, I went to the jail. The pigs wouldn't let me see Jimenez. TOOOT."

"What'd he do this time?"

"I don't know. I called Cecil. He'll look into it. TOOOT."

The couple sits for sixty vicious ticks of the clock. Each clock tick pierces Mort's skin like a tiny needle.

Angora wonders if she can stomach water. For a second, their minds sync up. Sweet Yadira was in the clutches of the CPS. Mort pictures her thick straight black hair; Angora can see the girl's nimble and mercurial arms, her exquisite hands.

"We have to get Yadira out of that place. Where's Silvia?"

"I don't know. TOOOT."

"Jimenez probably killed her."

"That's not funny. TOOOT."

Angora recalls the way Jimenez and Silvia used to caterwaul when they lived in the apartment upstairs. They would scream, moan or hump all hours of the night, every night, relentless passion in the service of pleasure. She suspected that Jimenez hit her when he lost control of his temper, she hated him for giving it and her for taking it.

"Remember when they first met?"

Mort laughs. He's back in Mexico with Jimenez. They'd been driving around Tijuana looking for a gig Solucion Mortal was supposed to be playing with Battalion of Saints, but got lost. They ended up at a bar on Revolucíon where you could get six beers for five American dollars in a metal bucket. Out on the dance floor, Jimenez met a girl who wanted a ride across the border.

"She says she walked a thousand miles to get here," Jimenez translated.

The woman, who looked about 18, didn't speak much English. She was from the southeastern part of Mexico and said her parents had been killed organizing coffee pickers. Full strong bloodshed. She was the most beautiful woman they had ever seen—with green eyes forged at the center of the earth. They got lucky and crossed the border without any hassles. On the way back they ducked into the South Bay drive-in and saw *Ghostbusters*. Mort sat in the front eating popcorn and sipping tequila while Silva and Jimenez made out in the back seat. The second picture in the double feature, *C.H.U.D.*, became "their movie" and Jimenez has seen it ten times since.

"I'm gonna shower."

Mort wants to join his wife. Does she know how beautiful she is? She prefers to bathe in isolation, needs quiet time to collect her thoughts, to meditate. He's watched her touch herself in the shower, one of the few places she could be by herself. He checks his desire to run soapy hands over her slender frame and goes to the kitchen to make coffee.

"You want coffee? TOOOT."

He hears her vomit into the toilet through the door. Her yellow puke splashes over the bowl and stirs up Mort's morning piss which makes her want to puke again. She has asked him repeatedly to flush the toilet. To hell with his stupid credo about saving water. Her bobbed hair points toward the floor. She contemplates, briefly, puking on the tile to avoid the stench. She remembers one time Mort stood over a pile of vomit and compared the colors and abstract slashes to Jackson Pollack. She married a fool. Her stomach dry hurls and sends a painful convulsion through tense abdominal muscles.

By the time she comes out of the shower, Mort clutches a phone in his right hand and a mug in his left. The lack of sleep reflects on his face. He looks old for twenty-seven, has the pallor of bleached bone. The furrow in his brow seems more pronounced, deeper. Less than a week ago, he got carded for a lottery ticket.

By the pouches under his eyes, he could swindle a senior discount at the movies. Dark half circles mark his face, one grossly darker where Angora socked him.

He looks dead.

"Cecil says we can pick up Yadira. They've got Jimenez on murder. TOOOT."

The stress that tears at the seams of Mort's forehead feels unbearable. He looks at his wife and wants to climb inside her. How nice it would be to curl up in her womb and disappear. He'd like to take out his kidneys, his lung, liver, heart, whatever can be donated, and sew it up inside her. He'd like to look at the world with his eyes through her brain.

"Oh my gosh! He did kill Silvia."

"They say he killed a cop. TOOOT."

"Oh my god. They say he did it." A rush of adrenaline shaves the edge off her hangover. "So, where's Silvia?"

They'd spent a lot of time together over the years, partying with or without occasion, seeing bands play in small clubs and just hanging out. Everybody loved Silvia. She was smart, beautiful and strong. She always knew what to do. She could organize any chaos thrown at her.

Mort would say their lives were entwined, "friends are thicker than blood," though to Angora they seemed but reflections in a mirror. They got pregnant around the same time. Jimenez was against marriage where Mort couldn't wait to tie the knot. Silvia had a job, so they had money to live, but she didn't breathe for her daughter the way Angora did for Cubby.

Angora sorts through these thoughts as she looks in on her son. Cubby's limbs are splayed out, he takes up the whole bed, Hula-hooping through a pastoral dream. Angora cannot recall a more beatific smile.

"Jimenez told Cecil that Silvia was deported. The INS came to the house; they kidnapped her, put her on a plane. TOOOT."

"So much for inalienable rights."

"Rights are for rich, white people. The governor plans to blame immigrants for crime or inflation to catapult himself to the White House. TOOOT."

"Doesn't she have a green card?"

"Thought so. Jimenez came home and saw them lead her out in handcuffs. Yadira was in the back seat of the car. He says his .45 wasn't in the glove box. He doesn't know what happened."

"Jimenez should have married her."

If they had thought to turn on the tv, another version of the story would have been presented.

A stout police captain stands in front of a small craftsman house outside a line of yellow caution tape and waits for the cue to make his statement. Cutaway to streets signs that show we are in the Barrio. Seven or eight patrol cars frame the image with colorful streaks of red and blue. The television crew throws a hot white light on the captain's face, so we can see he needs a shave and sleep, which deepens the shadows in the background.

An officer had been shot. The suspect's name is Jimenez Yaz. After resisting arrest, Yaz was taken to the MCC. A loaded gun, registered in his name, was found at the scene.

"No further comments at this time."

The news rehashes the incident at the top of every hour, experts speculate, look at it from a helicopter, interview neighbors and break for a shampoo commercial. Jimenez's arrest record paints him by numbers to be a dangerous criminal.

Mort leans into his wife. His need to pull together in this difficult moment manifests in an embrace. Her complaints have to be set aside, again. A reprieve like this can only be fleeting, so he soaks up every bit of warmth he can steal from her body. The copper-hued towel that wraps her torso brings out a new color in her eyes. His lips press into her wet hair.

"The life still there, upon her hair."

She feels him draw energy to recharge his battery for what lies ahead. She gives what she has, not much, and gets back his raw love. The raw love was never in question. But she needs action, safety and security. She needs progress rather than nostalgia. The towel slips. His mouth attaches to her nipple.

She still feels sick, but lets it go, giving as always giving. She thinks of sex as a gift. He presses her against the hall wall. It feels cold. Her feet come off the ground, fingers dig into a fleshy ass. His flaccid cock pumps at her vagina. The balls of her feet dig into the opposite wall. He grunts like a pig roots in the muck. The sex takes on the primordial rhythm of the swamps with the beat provided by his head BUMP against the wall over her shoulder. His chin nuzzles in the nape of her neck. His cock isn't hard enough. It doesn't matter.

BUMP BUMP BUMP.

## TWELVE

Negdin sits in a chair as old as he is. The variance in electrical charge between his agitated mind and the serene shroud of night pins him inexorably in the sticky web of insomnia. He hasn't slept much in three years. The moribund pain this particular morning seems more intense than usual. His back hurts less when he sits upright. His kidneys hurt less with the upper part of his body horizontal and the legs akimbo. The pain pill he swallowed about an hour before hasn't provided the advertised relief. His nervous system delivers messages like the kind you get from the dentist, the revenuers, the chaplain, the coroner.

He picks up one of the old magazines that fascinated Mort the day before, remembers reading Rube Goldberg's strips in the 30s after his mom ran off, trying like everyone in those days, not to get pulled down by The Great Depression.

He wanted to get up from the chair at sunrise. His muscles have so far resisted two weak attempts. That many hours in the same position contemplating death will do that. Eventually, the choked sunshine that sifts through the cracked drapes inspires Mr. Negdin to turn on his side and push with both hands, before he ambles across the room to the telephone.

He finds Mort's number on a scrap next to the phone. The old man dials the first numeral and lets his finger ride back in the hole. The next number, 9, has to be pulled around the dial. It saps a good part of his endurance.

"Hello. TOOOT."

"Hello, Mort?"

"This is Mort. TOOOT."

"You lost your mouthpiece."

"Oh, hello Mr. Negdin. TOOOT."

Mort walks into Cubby's room, carrying the phone. He kneels and searches under the bed.

"I can't wait much longer for that letter. This pain is nigh unbearable. Tonight…"

"You seemed like you were okay yesterday. TOOOT."

"You know Shinola about death and dying. Can you come over?"

"I'm not sure if I can make it today. TOOOT."

"What's wrong son?"

"My best friend was arrested. He called from jail last night. I've got to get his daughter from the authorities before they put her on a plane to Mexico City. TOOOT."

Mort finds the S-Device on a dirty sock between a balsa wood plane with a rubber band motor and an overturned Hot Wheels car. He dusts it off and pops it in his mouth. It tastes like a dirty sock.

"Well, uh, that takes precedent. Is there anything I can do?"

Here's a man ready to kill himself. He's lost the will to live, yet has the will to help a man he just met.

"If you can hold out."

"The mouthpiece. Mmm."

"It works. Your dad must have been a genius. I may have some time in the afternoon. The lawyer's taking care of my friend."

They hold on the line for a few seconds unsure what's left to be discussed. Negdin brushes a watery eye, hangs up the phone and walks to the green door. A spiral staircase winds down into the darkness. The pain has intensified. It sends amok jolts to parts of his body the old man had forgotten. When a bolt shoots into his cock, he thinks about his long-gone tumescence. He looks down at his dirty silk boxers. A man shouldn't die in filthy underwear.

The old geezer takes the steps slowly going deeper, deeper, he holds the handrail like a crutch. He breathes in stale air. He stops to rest half way, wants to head back up, but down feels easier. He tastes the dust on his lips. The faint light at the top of the stairs fades the deeper he winds into the basement. At the bottom, he's in total darkness and gropes the wall for the light switch. FLICK. A single bright incandescent bulb hanging from a frayed cord illuminates the scene.

The room contains an incredible machine.

Rube Goldberg might have designed it in the comic strips of yesteryear. Negdin collapses into a heavy wooden chair in the middle of it. A visual cacophony of wheels and pinions, wires and levers, pulleys and obscure gears link more familiar engines of personal destruction. A large caliber pistol clamped into position at Negdin's forehead. A hypodermic on a pendulum arm ready to swing into the fatty area of the buttocks. Razor sharp knives at rest above a set of steel arm clamps are destined to slit wrists. The needle is loaded with toxic fluid. An exhaust pipe extends out of a gas engine into what was once a gas mask from The First World War cleverly inverted for asphyxiation.

This was his father's master-invention. Negdin has oiled it, tuned it up and run tests for the day the machine could be put to use.

The suicide machine is comprised of brass, steel, wood and leather. The chair itself is carved from the stump of an olive tree. The electrodes attached to the seat and the wrist clamps are Leif's addition to his father's diabolical machine. He read somewhere that modern instruments of execution were outfitted with electricity. One must keep up with technology to stay relevant.

"Thanks Mort," he says out loud.

As the old man reposes on his throne, a death dream lifts his spirits from torment. This, he thinks, is only sleep.

Mort's Toyota pulls up in front of Negdin's house, around five in the afternoon. Before he can get up the walkway, he is greeted by a neighbor adjusting the sprinkler. The man is about twenty-five years younger than Negdin, bald, love-handled—a typical suburban animal.

"Hey, how you doing? I'm Chet King, you must be Negdin's son."

Mort nods his head, not interested in small talk.

"You'll have to excuse me; I've had a long day."

"When I saw you pull up yesterday, in that hearse, I figured Leif had gone to heaven."

Mort goes to the front door. The neighbor watches him crunch across the leafy walk. He pushes the bell. Whether it DING DONGS or BING BONGS is open to interpretation. He waits. Idles like a car at a stop sign. Chet waves.

Mort presses the bell again. His leg shakes, he feels anxious. He can't figure out why Chet bugs him. He runs a hand over the muscles in his neck, knocks three times hard. Anxious seconds pass. Mort tries the door and the knob turns. He hesitates before entering, steps off the porch into the house. The lights haven't been turned on. The room is dark. He feels for and finds a switch and the room lights up like a movie set.

The piles of discarded goods are amazing. Disoriented, he can't tell what's changed since his last visit. He spies the hourglass from the painting of Negdin's grandfather in a box with an old hat, a horseshoe, a hammer and what looks like a hairball from the stomach of an ox. The glass is broken, the sand run out. All of the windows in the house must be closed, the stuffy air makes it difficult to get a deep breath. It feels like drowning.

"Leif! Leif, are you here?"

He sees the green door—a "forest green" or more accurately the dapple-lighted green Monet captured in Camille's dress—which Negdin passed over during the tour. It stands ajar. A fly zips around Mort's sweaty forehead and prompts a futile swat. Maybe Negdin is another Bluebeard with bones in his basement. Finger bones, femurs, fibulas. Sacrums, skulls, scapulas and sesamoids.

The dim light from the front room reveals the first tread of the snake-like stairs. Mort steps cautiously, passing from light through darkness back to light in the basement. A figure slumps over in the chair. The silhouette of the pistol poised above. The monstrous shadow of the knives like the claws of some nightmarish beast.

"Mr. Negdin?"

The room feels stagnant. Mort strains his ears, begs his other senses to confirm his fear. He hears the faint BUZZ of a few flies. Smells shit. He steps into the room and ducks under the pulleys and levers and wires. He stands over the old man, reaches out a slow arm and rests his palm on Negdin's cold brow.

He's dead. His bowels must have released. Mort's eyes grow accustomed to the dim and trace the outline of a wet spot on the floor under Negdin's chair. A worried hand drags down the old man's face onto the sculpted French gothic bas-relief.

After a desolate minute, a remnant of Negdin's smiling face fades into memory. His closed eyelids red as heated metal. There doesn't seem to be any blood, any gore. The old man's shell is intact. The gun that points at the bowed head hasn't been fired. The knives are inert, unaware of the prey in their grasp. Mort walks around the machine, in awe of its unexercised potential. It could have scared the old man to death. He thinks of insect limbs, of mandibles. The assassin bug, the scorpion, the mantis, the centipede. Lovecraft, Giger, Cronenberg. He remembers watching a black widow wrap her dinner in tense white silk.

Mort circumnavigates the machine. Every screw, hinge and wedge, every axle and lever feels clean and cold and perfectly designed. Like an alien invasion raining down from the stars. The machine restores some power to dead words like "awesome," "marvelous," "fantastic" and "wonderful." Yet, none of these will do. It's so… very very.

Finally, he says, "It's full of scars."

He wants to draw it; he wants to paint it. He wants it to perform. He realizes he's always used art as a buffer against reality. Mort thought the old man would look serene in death, at peace, but any Stoicism has fallen away and the face is just blank.

He could be dead drunk in Giacometti's *City Square*.

Mort risks a finger on the arm of the hypodermic needle. He caresses the machine which returns a venerated spiritual foreboding. It should sit in a cathedral under a cupola of stained glass. He runs the finger across a knife blade surprised at how easily blood runs onto the palm of his hand.

He touches the old man again and the cold flesh repulses him. He feels scared. A dead man shouldn't be able to see you with his dead gray eyes. The house creaks and Mort wants out. A fly lands on the old man's elongated ear and rubs its filamentary tarsi lasciviously. Mort craves light. He thinks of Cubby. Of Yadira, cozy with Angora on the couch for a bedtime story. He thinks of her mother far away. He thinks of her father in jail.

Mort runs up the stairs and bangs his shin on the top step.

Out in the hallway, he expects Chet in the front room. What time is it? It feels like three o'clock in the morning. He feels like 3am day after day. Mort doesn't have a next move. Chet would call the police or an ambulance. Chet would scream for help. Mort turns a circle, sits on the floor in the hallway. He remembers the first time Angora dumped him. He sat in the shower, knees up to his chin, in the dark and let the water rain over his face. He doesn't remember if that was the first time he thought about it, suicide, but he changed or maybe broke. He was a different person after that. Maybe it was love, but it settled into him like a chemical oppression that never went away. Would he still banish love to end hate?

Mort's thoughts go crazy like white noise on tv!

Something deep inside the head and in the nerves cracks forth like a hissing screaming lobster, eeeeeeee. kkkkkkkkkkk.

One folded fist after another strikes the hard plaster wall. The skin on his knuckles peels away. He hits like a boxer on the heavy bag. Soon his head strikes the wall. BOMP BOMP. A font of blood gurgles out from the hairline. He bangs his head BOMP and again BOMP against the wall. He beckons a physical pain to match his thoughts.

He stumbles into the bathroom and stares at a picture of Jake LaMotta. Only it's the mirror, the battered nose of a pugilist emeritus. Arthur Craven beaten to a pulp by Jack Johnson. A wad of toilet paper jammed against the wound is quickly saturated. There's blood on his fingers. The rancid smell of Negdin's orange medicine piss in the toilet makes him feel sick. He pulls the chain and a weak rush of water carries some of it away.

Mort drags out his penis with one hand. The other presses the blood-soaked ball of toilet paper tighter against his head. He pisses. Washes his hands. Has to shit. He strains to push a thick log of shit out of his bowels into the toilet. He pushes so hard his rectum may come with it. The log fills the toilet like ice cream swirls in a cone.

He picks up a razor from the vanity. Van Gogh tugged at one ear with his left hand and severed it clean with a deft stroke of the right.

He paints the word "Bedlam" on the wall with the bloody cartilage swab.

Done with himself, he covers the spurting, so his brains won't fall out of his head, he turns on the shower, strips his clothes, unlaces the Dr. Marten boots—each angry finger throbs, he kills the light and sits under the cold but warming rain.

"Fuck this."

"Hey buddy, this chapter's over."

"Shut up. Shut the fuck up, Narrator. You're wasting water. I'm not your pawn or your puppet. You can't move me around the board like a game piece. You don't control me."

"I won't write exposition for this."

"I can narrate my own life. I'm rinsing the residue of shit off my ass. I'm getting out of this shower. Shutting it off. I'm naked. The water is dripping off my hairy body. A big puddle, a medium-sized puddle, a small puddle getting smaller and finally wet footprints walking down the hall. Down two, three steps at a time. I'm back in the basement with the old dead guy."

"Hey, don't touch that body, PT is supposed to come over and help you put it in the hearse."

"Shut up. I don't follow scripts. This old guy's death is supposed to help me realize it's a meaningful life? Who is he? Obi Wan Kenobi? Who am I? I got some news for you… Jimmy Stewart should have jumped! Fuck you. I'm picking up the dead body and dumping it on the floor. His carcass is heavier than it looks. His corpse THUMPS as it hits the brick. Stiff with rigor mortis. Bent in a seated position. Okay, I'm sitting in the wooden chair inside this contraption. Fuck it. I never wanted this job. I was born dead. Okay my arms are clamped down, wrists up. I push button (A) which releases lever (B) which triggers pulley (C) which sets in motion arm (D) which simultaneously causes pistol (E) to fire, knives (F) to slit my wrists, needle (G) to inject poison into my ass (H) An… N—

## THIRTEEN

Angora sits in the center of the couch with Cubby and Yadira's heads at rest in her lap while she reads from Art Spiegelman's *Maus*, which Mort had started a few days before. When the kids zonk out, she repeats the page number to herself several times in lieu of a bookmark. She holds each child as if a breeze might sweep them away. It feels selfish to absorb so much comfort. This was all she had ever wanted.

Angora recalls that Cubby as an infant bit her nipples raw so the areola dried up and scabbed over. She pumped her milk, but the contraption left her sore as well, so she weaned him onto a bottle as soon as he was ready. How strange to have nostalgia for a job you never liked doing. An hour has passed since the kids fell asleep and Mort hasn't returned from his "job."

After the phone RINGS, it RINGS twice more before she can scoot from under the sleeping babes, careful to set each child's head on a pillow.

"Hello."

"Hola Angora, it's me Jimenez."

"Hi. Where are you?"

"I'm not sure; they move me around. Ahh. I only have a minute."

"What's going on?"

"I'm waiting for arraignment. I met with the lawyer. Is Yadira there? Is she safe?"

"Yadira is here, she's asleep, peacefully."

"Thank you so much."

"It's okay. She's an angel."

"I don't know what's gonna happen to her mother. I don't know what's gonna happen to me. Promise you'll take care of mi pequeña comerada."

Angora's eyes, fixed on the girl, admire her perfect, brown skin and the eyelashes—so thick they could be used as brooms.

"Of course. Like my own. Mort too. You know that."

"I'm worried about Mort."

"Jimenez, you're in jail accused of killing a cop and you're worried about Mort? He's never been good at pressure, but he can handle it."

The phone cuts off.

Angora lays blankets over the children and goes to the bathroom. The tile feels cold on her bare feet. Her jeans slide to the floor, she kicks them off, bends to pick them up, folds them. She lifts the hood of the toilet seat, drops her panties around her ankles. Legs spread apart, the thumb and index finger of her right hand pinch the white string that dangles from her vagina. The blood-sticky tampon slides right out. Brownish-red blood saturates the water. The future looks bleak. There's no plan.

Angora's hair remains precise, hanging straight down like an elegant lamp shade.

Her body wants sleep but her mind is wracked with anxiety. She puts Cubby's sneakers in his room, picks up Yadira's Mary Jane's and runs a finger over the patent leather. She had these shoes when she was eight. She puts them in Cubby's room too. There's a Trevor Hoffman poster on the wall, toy trucks under the bed. The dresser doesn't seem big enough for Yadira's clothes. She wants her to feel like part of the family. In the aluminum room, Angora picks up the mug Mort left behind and stretches to pick up his pen on the floor. The cushion on the green chair is cocky-wampus.

She puts it straight and sees Mort's notebook. She picks it up together with her wig. She recalls the times she'd found his car keys in the chair after he "looked everywhere" and wonders what else has slipped between the cracks. She isn't prepared.

Angora usually avoids reading the unadulterated thoughts Mort sets down in these notebooks, but she feels it's worth the risk. She finds a rough copy of the suicide letter Mort wrote for Negdin.

Mort's words paint the image of an old man whose life was masoned from bricks of pain. How did he capture this guy so well? He knew him for, what, a day? At the bottom Mort wrote, "I don't blame anyone for it, it wasn't your fault." She's never felt anyone's pain like this, but still… in the end she can't understand his will to die.

Downtown, the Xmas lights remind her of the season. Angora hasn't done any shopping. They need a tree. Some midwinter festivity. She'll have to find the box of ornaments. She conjures the smell of pine needles and drifts into a dark dream that the old man in the suicide note is Mort.

# FOURTEEN

Angora stretches across the mattress to silence the alarm at 6am. Work! Her tired feet carry her deadweight across the hardwood floor. The children remain as she left them asleep on the couch. Mort should be in Cubby's bed. That's where she'd find him after a night out to see a band.

"I didn't want to disturb your slumber, Honey."

The Speed Racer comforter on Cubby's bed is spread flat, tucked in, like the calm water in the harbor outside the window.

Angora washes her hands and her face with the special face soap. She brushes her teeth, takes the floss out of the cabinet. She saws between each tooth and wipes the bits of food material on her finger. Washes again before she leaves the bathroom.

"Where the fuck is Mort?"

Why does he always have to flake like this?

The children are asleep, she feels segregated in the conscious world.

"Maybe I should call the police?"

She crawls back into bed, pulls the quilt over her head.

Around 9am, Cubby and Yadira discover each other awake.

"Hey Cubby, are there any cartoons on? Let's watch *Caspar* or *Scooby Doo*!"

"I don't think so. My dad only lets me watch on Saturday morning."

"What's going to happen to my dad?"

"He'll be okay. My dad will help him get out of jail."

"Maybe we can bust him out."

"We might have to."

"My dad didn't kill that police officer. I woke up when I heard the gunshot, but my dad was already handcuffed."

Her father talked about the police a lot. He usually called them "bastards" or "pigs" or "the army of the rich." He'd say, "I don't have to show you any stinking badges, you god-damned cabrón" in a funny voice to show he had a sense of humor about it, but she knew he didn't trust them like the cop who visited their school said you should.

"Oye! Pequeña camarada, remember, a cop will always eat the last donut."

Her mother would kiss her on the forehead and pull apart the last cookie or divide the last concha in parts to share.

"Don't be a little pig, mija. There are other people in the world."

Yadira bites a fingernail.

"Are you okay Yadira?"

"No."

Cubby shifts his position to hug her. His short arm is barely long enough to get a good grip. She clasps onto his PJs. Her tiny eight-year-old fingernails need the polish removed.

"It'll be okay."

Cubby plants a kiss on her forehead. Yadira tries not to cry. Cubby attempts a second kiss, this time on her nose, which feels slimy.

"Oooo."

"Sorry."

His third strikes her on the lips. Neither of them had kissed anyone lip to lip. Cubby isn't sure about it. Yadira is sure it's gross. She leans her tiny body into his and tries to kiss him back, but his tongue slips over the barrier of lips into her mouth. They taste each other's spit.

"Cubby."

"Yeah?"

"I'm sorry but it's yucky."

"Agreed."

"What's that poking me?"

"I don't know, where?"

"Down there."

The feeling brings on a near gone memory of the time she found her mother's "back massager."

"Yadira, what are you doing?"

"Hey Mama, you gotta try this."

She didn't understand why her mother had laughed so hard. She knows about "privates" and knows the reason they're private has to do with sex. No one would call her family sheltered. An interviewer once described her mother as a "sexual revolutionary" because she wore a t-shirt that said, "Feminists Fuck Better."

She's been to the zoo a hundred times puzzled by the way bears do it and turtles and the creatures on the "Hoof and Horny Mesa" seem to be constantly engaged in procreation.

"Lemme see."

Yadira lifts the blanket.

"But wait!"

Cubby produces the Green Ranger plastic action figure from where he'd been hiding it and zooms it toward Yadira.

"SHHHEEW! Rangers of power!"

He xylophones her ribs with the plastic action figure and they giggle together at full volume. She shakes free and cuffs Cubby with a pillow. She leaps on him like a professional wrestler off the top rope. Cubby picks up a pillow and whacks her in turn.

Angora startles awake and leaps out of bed. She surges into the living room in time to catch Yadira hop on each of two cushions across the couch and bounce over to the coffee table with her pillow poised for attack.

"What are you kids up to?"

"Nothing."

Yadira's pillow connects over Cubby's lowered guard.

Angora opens her arms and the kids charge into her with two delicious morning hugs.

"What's for breakfast?"

"Cereal."

"Where's Dad?"

"I don't know. Cubby, you get the cereal bowls, I'll get the milk. Yadira you fold the blankets."

Where the hell is Mort?

RINGGGGG! Angora nearly pours the milk over the table. Cubby picks up the phone.

"Hi, Cubby, is your dad there?"

"No, my dad's not here." He shakes his head—negative—to the question.

"My mom's here. It's Lilli."

"Hi, Lilli. Have you seen Mort?"

Yadira stuffs a big bite of cereal into her mouth. The milk drips onto her chin.

"Not recently. He came in the other day with this crazy idea…"

"About a suicide business, I know. It's ghastly. He went to the old man's house last night and didn't come back."

"That's why I called. PT went down to the Hemlock Society and hung up some flyers for the "D-M-S-D" and the phone has been ringing off the hook."

"DSM—?"

"Death Museum Suicide Division."

"It's been crazy around here. This whole suicide note idea is reprehensible, it's awful. Isn't suicide against the law?"

One of the cereal bowls crashes on the kitchen floor. The kids stampede into the living room.

"Just a second Lilli."

"It was her fault Mom."

"No, it was your fault."

"I don't care whose fault, help each other clean it up. And be careful not to cut yourselves… I'm sorry Lilli, what did you say?"

"It's been crazy. Every disconsolate loon in the world called. They want eulogies and obituaries too. There's a woman who wants to pay ten thousand dollars for one of Mort's suicide notes."

"Ten thousand dollars? BEEP. Hold on, that's my other line."

"Hi, hi."

"Hey, Squeaky, let me call you back."

"Do you wanna go to the gym?"

"I can't…"

"Okay. Call me back."

Angora clicks back to Lilli; the line is dead.

She doesn't know Lilli's number; nor does she want to spend fifty cents on *69 to reverse the call. That's a full load of laundry. She walks over to the aluminum room and searches through the piles of books and papers for Mort's address book. She feels discouraged. Coffee!

Yadira wields a broom; Cubby crouches with the dustpan.

"Ouch."

"Sorry, I didn't do it on purpose."

An only child, Angora doesn't have experience with sibling rivalry. Short of killing each other, she supposes, Yadira will be good for Cubby.

"Give me the broom."

"No, I'm the sweeper."

"What's wrong with your mama now?"

"Our parents are going crazy."

"Maybe we should run away."

"Maybe you should clean up that mess."

She removes another tampon soaked with her dark menses. She remembers the period where Mort wanted to use her bodily excretions in a sculpture. That was the day she lost interest in art.

He glued used condoms to a canvas. He picked snot soiled tissues from the waste paper basket. He and Cubby wiped ear wax and boogers on the piece for months. She incinerated it one day when Mort went to the unemployment office. He called her a "fascist."

"Where the hell is Mort?"

RINGGGGG! RINGGGGG!

"Cubby!"

He drops the dustpan and spills pieces of the broken bowl.

"Hello."

"Hi."

"Hi, Cubby, this is Renata. Is your mom there?"

"Yeah, she's in the bathroom."

"Oh… Ask her if she's coming into work today."

"Mom! Are you going to work?"

"No!"

"She says no."

"Is anything wrong?"

"A few things, bye."

# FIFTEEN

Nix steams milk for a latte with his left hand, claps out the coffee grounds from the portafilter and loads the machine for another shot with his right. His spiky blue hair looks greasy. The mop of hair smells like old clothes and blueberry. Renata makes change for a fifty and answers questions about the fat content in a whole milk mocha. The tip jar contains eight dollars and fourteen cents.

The man in the tan suit is back.

"Aaaaahh!" He shrieks and to no one in particular says, "You people ought to warn us about how hot this coffee is!"

Nix looks around. Renata had said "not to bother" with the latte art, since most of the customers preferred their drinks fast to pretty, but he thought the man in tan suit might appreciate the simple tulip. He'd gotten in a fight at a vegan hardcore gig the night before, evident by a bruised eyelid, and wasn't in the mood to take any shit.

"I'm a lawyer, I know my rights."

Nix looks at Renata who has made forty-two espressos in the first three hours of today's shift. She had restocked the Styrofoam cups before the shop opened and there were only a few left. They were soaked in sweat. The other person who was supposed to be working had already been gone 30 minutes on her 15-minute break. Nix has the feeling Renata doesn't want to apologize because he wouldn't want to. How many times can one person say "Sorry" in a day? It's like dragging a dead horse through the world.

"It's coffee idiot. Of course, it's hot."

"Excuse me?"

"I said coffee is a hot drink and you're a moron!"

His comment raises a few chuckles from the customers in line. Most laugh because the comeuppance was unexpected and a few because they felt uncomfortable.

"I am a paying customer young man. You have no right to speak to me like that."

Nix unties his apron. His knuckles are already swollen from last night's squab at the show. The apron smells like a balmy dairy, since he hasn't had a chance to wash it.

A disembodied voice over the intercom says, "Dr. Black, seventh floor," which prompts the hospital security guard to pick up his radio and walk across the lobby to the elevator.

"Excuse me miss. Aren't you the manager? I need to file another complaint."

Nix waits until the elevator closes on the security guard and steps around the front of the espresso bar.

"Let me hold this for you."

Nix takes the cappuccino out of the man's hand. He removes the lid, dips his finger into the coffee and lets a few drops fall onto his wrist like a mother testing a bottle.

"You're right, it is hot."

"Just leave me alone."

Nix hands the cup back to the man in the tan suit who—and no one saw this coming—flings the hot liquid onto the young barista, soaking his uniform shirt and trousers. Some of the people in line thought the man looked indignant, as if his privilege was being challenged. At least one person thought it was a nervous accident. Everyone but the man in the tan suit saw the consequences would be swift and brutal.

The first punch, a left, catches the man with the tan suit on the throat. His collapsing trachea forces him to sputter and gasp for breath as he drops to his knees. One of the other customers kicks the fallen customer in the ass. A sharp kick from a steel-toed boot follows and Nix continues to kick the man in the tan suit until the skin peels from his scalp and exposes a bright and bloody patch of bone.

Most of the witnesses say, as they retell the story again and again with their own air punches and feigned kicks, that the severity of the beating was excessive. A doctor lifts his double espresso from the bar. He hopes the man with the tan suit has health insurance.

"It's a good thing he got beat up in a hospital."

Nix breathes heavily. He pulls the wet shirt off and wraps it around his throbbing fist.

"Sorry Renata, but that guy bugged me."

She doesn't know how to react. A bit of nervous energy compels her to pick up a rag and wipe up some crumbs from the counter that had fallen off of a blueberry scone.

Someone says, "The prick deserved it."

Nix smiles dumbly. The tan suit is wrinkled and soiled with blood.

"Do you want me to make that macchiato?"

"No, why don't you take the rest of the morning off."

"Could I get my share of the tips?"

"Yeah sure."

The customer who'd kicked the man in the tan suit stuffs a dollar into the tip jar.

SIXTEEN

Angora paces the hardwood floor in her living room. She yearns for guidance from the universe. Some direction. Any random sign would help. Cubby and Yadira play with action figures in the bedroom. She tries the radio—an NPR reporter describes an atrocity in Uganda. Angora turns the dial. Mexican music. Styx. Pop R & B. Commercials. Alternative. Classical. More commercials. Dead air. Some religious bullshit. Another Mexican station. She flips the radio off.

Outside the clouds look heavier than brushed aluminum—a cruel but idle threat of rain. Angora wants coffee. Mort always makes it for her. She loads the espresso maker with ground beans and water. Flicks the switch. She opens the refrigerator.

"Shit."

She runs a hand through her hair. A divine aroma rises on the steam as the coffee pushes out of the HISSING machine. She only drinks coffee with milk.

"Where is Mort?"

He could be at the Death Museum. He could have fucked off to Mexico. Angora wants to call the lawyer. She worries about the dead cop. His wife and children cried in front of the news cameras.

Knock.

Angora looks through the peephole. Nix smiles at her dumbly. She notes his blackened eye, his sweaty naked chest and the T-shirt wrapped around his hand.

"What happened to you?"

"I got this shiner at a gig. Some skinheads started shit."

"Oh."

"And I burned my hand on some hot coffee at work."

"Wait, what are you doing here?"

"I looked up your address."

"Yeah?"

"I thought you might want to hang out."

His pants sag despite the studded leather belt. Cubby and Yadira emerge from the bedroom.

"Who's at the door, Mom?"

"You have kids?"

"This is Nix. He works at the espresso bar."

"Are you a punker? My dad says teenagers don't know shit about punk rock."

"I'm not a punker, just a punk."

"Where'd you get that Black Flag tattoo?" Yadira asks. "Jail?"

"Come on in and sit down."

Nix sits in the green chair.

"So, what's up?"

"Oh my gosh. So much shit… Do you want to hear about it?"

"Sure. I got no place to go."

"Do you want some coffee?"

"As long as it's not cappuccino."

She carries the cold espresso in from the kitchen. The cup is too full and a little coffee beats the rim.

"Have you got any sugar?"

"Yes, but no milk."

"I hate milk."

"Mort hates milk too."

"Who's Mort?"

An hour later, Nix wrestles with the kids in the yard. He has Yadira on his back and Cubby in a headlock. He used to say he didn't like children, but these kids were fun.

Circle Jerks blast out of the CD player with Keith Morris singing:

*I don't wanna live, to be forty-three. I don't like, what I see going on around me…*

Yadira climbs the tree in the front yard and shouts from the branches.

"You can't catch me. You can't catch me."

Nix covers his face when she throws a fig. A rotten piece of fruit fragments—explodes in juice, gnats and fruit meat.

"Yaack!"

Angora steps out of the kitchen to check on the commotion as her son hits Nix with a torrent from a squirt gun. He remembers why he disliked children. Another fig smacks him on the cheek.

"Rrrrrgggg!"

He rattles the tree like King Kong as Yadira goes for a higher branch and misses a step—the gray sky recedes as she falls. She thinks, "I wonder what it will be like to hit the ground?" Fortunately, Nix is there to catch her in outstretched arms before she can find out.

Angora steps back to the kitchen to stir the pot of spaghetti. She minced garlic and tossed in an onion. Cubby likes his noodles without sauce but Yadira isn't picky. She eats like a grizzly.

"She scraped her arm on the tree."

"She'll be okay. Do you want a Band-Aid sweetie? Would you like to stay for dinner?"

"Sure. I'll run to the corner store for ice cream."

"Can you grab some milk?"

"Mom, where's Dad?"

"I don't know, Honey."

•••

A fly buzzes around the hole in Mort's skull before dropping like a helicopter into the maw of a volcano. Landing on the brain tissue, the fly takes nourishment and deposits 150 eggs. Mort's face is solemn in death, his buttocks blackened where the needle stuck. Dried blood coats the arm restraints and the floor around the chair.

Negdin's corpse decays where Mort had pushed it onto the floor.

Outside, Chet waters his lawn.

•••

Nix finishes the last bit of ice cream and stacks the dishes. He licks the bowl clean. He holds his hands under a stream of hot water and washes them with care.

Angora watches Winona Ryder in *The Crucible*. She wants to take her mind off Mort and the cop and Jimenez and Silvia. The dishes clank in the kitchen.

"You kids get ready for bed. PJs on and teeth brushed."

A minute later, the two kids giggle in the bathroom. Yadira runs out in front of the tv, her mouth foamed with toothpaste.

"He farted. He farted."

"Go back and rinse your mouth, before you get toothpaste all over everything. I'll comb your hair."

"It stinks in there."

Angora pauses the video and runs the brush through Yadira's thick black hair. The flowers have failed in the jelly jar. A closeup of John Proctor's troubled face fills the screen.

"Thanks Mama."

A slip. Wow, that felt amazing. She wipes the tear that forms in the corner of her eye. Mort resisted having more kids. His obstinance drove her insane.

"It wouldn't be fair to the parents in China. It wouldn't be fair to the Earth. Why do you want another kid? We got it right the first time."

"Go on to bed now sweetie. Tomorrow, I'll paint your fingernails."

"Cool."

"Hey, that's my bed."

"Mine now."

"Cubby, stop it. You two can share."

"Can you leave the light on?"

"It's okay sweetheart. I'll be right here watching tv."

"Mom, why does dad always say, 'Kill your television, before it kills you?'"

"Go to bed, Honey."

She pulls the door closed, leaving it ajar and remembers how upset Mort was about the tv Jimenez bought Cubby for his birthday.

"When you're watching tv or playing video games you are in another world. It's like you're dead but you're not dead. You're away, you're undead."

"Nah, homie. You gotta kill the cop in your mind. That's your predicament. The chavalitos who play the same games and watch the same shows have a connection with their peers. Our whole generation is glued together by *Chico and the Man, Mork & Mindy*. Different strokes for different folks. You teach 'em to pick the corn out the bullshit."

They kept the tv over Mort's objections because Angora missed talking to people at work about all her favorite shows.

Nix stands, framed by the door and holds a towel.

"I finished the dishes."

"That's sweet."

He smiles kind of dumbly.

"Do you want to watch the movie?"

John Proctor looks at him from the tv.

"Maybe I should go."

"I'd rather have company. You could stay 'til Mort shows up."

"What do you think happened?"

"Knowing him… Should I call the police?"

"I don't like cops much."

Angora hits play and John Proctor resumes his anguished lament. Angora wishes it was that simple to put pain on hold. Nix unlaces his steel-toed boots, pulls them off and lets each CLUMP on the hardwood floor. He wads his dirty socks in a ball, sniffs and stuffs them into one of the boots.

RINGGGGG!

Nix likes how Angora's hairstyle retained composure throughout the chaotic day. He was about to tell her so when the phone rang.

"Hello."

"Hi, Angora, it's Lilli. Any word from Mort?"

"Nope. Can I get your number?"

Angora writes the number on Mort's notebook.

"Have you guys got any idea where this old man lives?"

"He didn't say where. We need to find him. The lady called."

"About the ten thousand?"

"Yep. PT and I thought about writing the suicide note for her, but we know you and Mort need the money."

"Mort hasn't worked in a year."

"Artists are like that."

People always sympathize with his selfish priorities. Silvia and Jimenez did it even while they were buying a house and a new car.

"If you hear anything, give me a call. I'm worried."

"Okay. We will."

"Ow."

Nix leans over and pries free part of a tooth from his bare foot.

"What's this?"

"Uh..."

"It looks like a tooth."

"It could be."

Nix leans forward to kiss her. Angora tastes his firm, aggressive lips as he swings on top of her lap and sucks at her neck in a fever. He licks and slurps like a hyena at the innards of a fresh kill. Angora kisses his swollen black eye and strokes his pimply face. He makes his way down her neck onto the breasts, saliva soaks the thin material of her tank top and turns on her nipples. He smells a bit rancid, his blue hair like old clothes with a faint tincture of blueberry. He slips onto the floor between her legs and rubs his forehead against her pubic bone. His chin and forehead push the sanitary napkin under her jeans up into her crotch and back into her butt crack. The young boy's swollen fingers fumble with the button fly to her jeans.

"Please stop. I can't do this."

On the tv, the first witch is pushed off the scaffold—the fall snaps her neck and the knot that chokes off circulation to the brain feels like overkill.

## SEVENTEEN

On Mondays, the Death Museum opens at noon, so PT likes to wake up early and take the hearse to the car wash. He details the car himself, vacuums the interior and polishes the chrome. Once a month, he rubs formaldehyde into the leather seats.

The hearse is kept in a downtown parking structure, of gray concrete like a Brutalist mausoleum, under 24-hour surveillance. He drove her Thursday, the day before Mort borrowed it for the "business excursion."

In the garage, PT deactivates the alarm BEEP BOOP, unlocks the door, disengages the kill switch, unhitches The Club and puts the key in the ignition.

He has to readjust the seat and change the position of the mirrors. A turn of the key releases a wild, mind erasing discord of windshield wipers dry humping the windshield DUDUDUDUD, flashing left turn signal TICKTICK TICK TICK, the heater blowing HWOAAAAAAA! behind a howling blast of sound from the stereo:

*More suicides please…*

"Mort, you fucking joker. Ha ha. If you believe you've lived your life the right way, you've got nothing to fear."

Resetting the knobs, switches and volume control restores serenity to the hearse and the parking garage. PT flips the tape over. Bauhaus comes on with less volume as Peter Murphy sings:

*They came from next door.*

PT puts the cassette case back in the glove compartment and notices a letter from Timothy McVeigh he meant to get framed for the museum.

He crumples a scrap of paper on the seat into a tiny ball and flicks it out the window.

"Mort's such a pig."

PT turns to the back and says, "Sorry Bedlam" to the giant pig stretched out on his belly above the fold-down jump seats.

"Still no word from Mort?" Lilli says into the phone.

"No, he was trying the other day though, he brought flowers… I'm thinking about calling the police."

"I know a cop, who comes in here. Do you want me to call him?"

"That would be great."

Lilli can hear the kids run through the house in the background. She loves animals—buries roadkill, rescues possums in distress, saves baby hummingbirds that have fallen out of nests and takes in strays when she can, but has never considered raising human children of her own.

"Any word about Jimenez? I saw it on the news."

"Leave me alone!"

"Lilli, I gotta go take care of these kids."

Lilli twiddles a pencil. She taps it four times on the notepad. Closer inspection reveals a faint impression where Mort copied down the directions to the old man's house. She rubs the pencil across the paper to raise the hidden message. She'd seen this trope on tv and remembers Hitchcock using it in a film. She loves true crime and hardboiled fiction and has read everything by Raymond Chandler and Jim Thomson.

The number 1332 emerges.

•••

The flies continue to multiply exponentially around Mort's corpse. His face looks heavily creased and what's left of his brain is like a fish bowl for a swimming soup of maggots as his eyeballs come to dissolution in their sockets. The flies have found their way into Negdin too. The collective BUZZ sounds like an electrical transformer.

Chet is at work.

•••

Three tourists, German by their accent, come into the museum. The guy's head is blade-shaved close to the skull. The girls' have Chelsea bobs with fringe bangs. Their polo shirts and pressed trousers could be mistaken for a uniform. The dude wears Levi's 501s, not yet washed, so, very dark blue and a green bomber jacket.

"Oi. Would you be interested in any Nazi paraphernalia?"

"What you got, bro?"

The girls leaf the pages of *Murder Can Be Fun*, *Genetic Disorder* and *Answer Me!* picked off the glass display case that holds one of Stewart Home's "Necro Cards," a signed copy of *Hollywood Babylon*, a plaster cast of Jimi Hendrix's penis, John Dillinger's death mask and a beaked-mask worn by a doctor in the time of the Black Plague. There's a cartoon about pilgrims to the "new world" hanging a boy who fornicated with sheep. The shorter skinhead points while the other smirks.

"A friend of mine from East Berlin has wild stuff."

"Like Hitler's foreskin?"

"I've got a couple of Jew balls," the skinhead says and gestures to the jars of animal testicles displayed on the counter.

PT looks the skinhead in the eye. He doesn't like fascists, but can show tolerance for anyone who pays to enter the museum.

"He means between his legs," one of the girls says. "Erich, show him your tattoos."

The skinhead lifts his shirt. A giant Star of David covers the breadth of his chest above a word in Hebrew letters. "Never Forget" is stenciled on his wrist.

"Our friend's got SS badges, a dagger with a swastika and evil shit like that."

The skinhead slaps the Ace of Spades on the counter, a business card with his name and number printed on the back.

"I'll think about it, bro."

"The kids in Atari Teenage Riot told me about this place."

"Yeah. We took some rad pictures of them posed in the coffins."

"How much is it to go down into the museum?"

"It's five bucks."

"Let's get out of here, Erich."

"Next time," the skinhead says. PT and Lilli watch the trio walk down the street.

"It's always entertaining. Oh. Oh look. I found a clue to Mort's disappearance. The old man's address."

"He's probably out fucking some chick."

"PT? We're talking about Mort."

"He's probably out fucking some dude."

"Ha ha, very funny." She slides the notepad across the counter.

"Can't read the street name."

PT walks back to the refrigerator, lifts a cold green bottle, pries the top with an opener, sets the opener in the human skull they use as a catchall for pens, scissors, a hole punch, paper clips and ammonia snaps. He takes a swig.

"Maybe Mort left his copy of the directions in his pants pocket."

"I'll call Angora." Lilli dials and the phone rings but cuts off when PT puts his finger on the switch hook. "What?"

PT swallows a gulp of Heineken.

"He left the directions in the hearse."

"Awesome!"

"Fuck."

"What?"

"I tossed them out the window."

"Come on."

What light there is in the parking garage is dim, gray and shadowy. The couple hold hands as they descend a spiral ramp toward the hearse. Lilli's tango heels clop like hooves on the cement.

UH UH UH UH UH

"What's that?"

The few cars in the garage appear to be empty. The sound gets louder as they proceed down the ramp.

UH PAP UH PAP UH PAP

"Sounds like animals fucking."

They turn the final cement column where the hearse is parked and stalk like deer hunters through the trees.

UH PAP UH PAP UH PAP

"What is that?"

"Sounds like balls banging against ass cheeks."

The woman's legs point up to the cement ceiling. She wears high heels, the kind that click when she walks to let people know she's coming. The man has short black hair and a hairy ass.

UH PAP UH PAP UH PAP

"They're right next to the hearse."

"Such a bold display of freedom."

"Oh yeah."

PAP PAP PAP UH UH UH

UH UH UH PAP PAP PAP

PT and Lilli stand over the sex show.

"They have interesting bodies."

"Would you call this a public display of affection?"

"In extremis."

"Nice technique though."

"Ya, they know. Life is short, you have to appreciate every…"

"…thrust."

"I was going to say 'moment,' but 'thrust' works."

UH PAP UH PAP UH PAP

The woman's blonde hair rustles like a burning palm tree in a warm Santa Ana wind.

UH PAP UH PAP UH PAP

PT reaches down and picks up the wadded paper.

"Did you hear that?" the blonde says.

The man with the short black hair sort of grunts Mmmm.
He changes up the rhythm from thrust to nudge to lunge,
but doesn't or can't say a word.

EIGHTEEN

Cubby searches under the bed for his right sneaker.

"Mom, why do we have to go to school?"

"I don't feel like going either, Angora."

The children wear matching uniforms—blue pants, white shirts.

"Found it!"

Sand pours over the Speed Racer comforter as he holds the found shoe aloft.

"I need you guys to go to school, so I can get some things done… Plus you need an education."

"A free babysitter."

"Don't get smart with me young man."

Angora tries the radio. Broom in hand, she pushes a dust ball out of the corner into a pile in the center of the room. Hair, flakes of human skin and stuff tracked in on the bottom of shoes nest in enough sand to start a beach. A "Please Remove Your Shoes" sign might help. Mort said he would put a little bench outside the door for visitors. Mort says a lot of things. Cubby and Yadira could be made to comply, but retraining Mort, who only takes his boots off before a shower, would be difficult.

"It's too much hassle, what if I have to go out to buy milk?"

How many times had she unlaced those stupid boots as he slept on the couch?

RINGGGGG!

"Hello."

"Hey, Angora. I called my friend on the force and he said don't worry. People go missing all the time. I found an address we could check out though."

She'd never felt comfortable around PT and Lilli. They seemed a little wild, a little dangerous. She'd spoken with Lilli more in the last three days than the last three years.

"Can you pick me up? Mort took the car."

"Okay, PT's gonna stay here and open the museum. See you soon."

Lilli glides the hearse up to the curb. The Stooges *Death Trip* plays on the stereo. Angora waits with her arms folded across her chest; a black purse slung over one shoulder. She wears sensible shoes, at least compared to Lilli's tango heels. Lilli steps out of the hearse wearing dark sunglasses and black plastic pants. She teeters around to the passenger side. Angora notes the metal stud through her navel.

"Hey, Honey. You ready for a little adventure."

"Mort better have a good explanation."

Lilli opens the heavy door of the Cadillac. Angora sits on the passenger side while Lilli teeters around to take her place in the driver's seat.

"PT threw the directions out the window in the parking garage and this horny lady who was fucking her boyfriend in the garage used the paper for a gum wrapper. When we picked the gum off, it took most of the street name."

"So now what?"

"PT did the math. He always clocks the mileage on the hearse, and uh, he also noticed how many songs had cycled through on the cassette and considering how fast Mort drives, plus you said Mort brought flowers, which, knowing him means a detour to pick them off a grave at Mt. Hope. So, PT used a compass to draw a circle in the Thomas Brothers guide, by dead reckoning, the street is 'Taylor Way' or 'Taylor Drive'. One is in El Cajon and one near the cemetery."

"Mt. Hope is closer."

"Buckle up, arrive alive."

Recalling the grisly photographs of car wrecks in the museum—black and white brains splattered across red asphalt—Angora clicks the seatbelt.

As the hearse glides along the road, Angora daydreams about Mort. She pictures a house. She knows he's inside. He could be in bed with another woman; he could be dead. Both seem true.

Lilli thinks about the old man on the phone. Even though our culture is obsessed with death, most people don't think about it. So, Negdin must not be most people. PT says mediocre souls consider life and death separate. He doesn't worry about it more than birth or old age. Since death is a farce none of us endure first hand, there's no reason to fear it. She is unsure. Exhibits from the walls of the museum flash through her thoughts—Sharon Tate on the floor, Jim Jones at the Housing Authority, the insane couple who took the film of a murder they did to get developed at the Fotomat.

She notices Siouxsie and the Banshees version of *Helter Skelter* playing through the stereo. She turns up the volume as Siouxsie sings:

> *…you may be a lover but you ain't no fucking dancer…*

"I remember when Mort made this tape for you," Angora says, raising her voice above the music. "He sorted through a hundred songs. He was trying to decide between *Code Blue* by TSOL and *Last Caress* by The Misfits. You know The Misfits have the hair that goes down their face."

"Devilocks."

"That's it. We listened to the songs a bunch of times. They're both disgusting. *Code Blue* is about a guy who has sex with dead bodies. And The Misfits say things like 'I killed your baby today' and 'I raped your mother.' Mort thought it was about Vietnam. Soldiers killing babies and raping women in the back country. That's what war is, he said. But then the song goes, 'It doesn't mean that much to me,' which makes me think it's about us. About our indifference. Like we don't feel it."

"That's why we started the museum. People see so many fake murders in movies and on TV, it doesn't mean much. We show the real thing, so they have to think about it."

A black cat darts into the street and Lilli slams the brakes.

"Is she okay?"

"Ya, there she goes."

"1332 Taylor Drive. That's it across the street."

The hearse eases up in front of a house with palm trees and telephone lines out front. Most of the houses look like temporary bungalows thrown up for military families in the 1940s. The electrical boxes are tagged with graffiti. A sneaker dangles from the wire. Seven or eight crows look on. The address matches one on the side of a pale blue cottage. There doesn't appear to be anybody home. On the porch, a swing with a rusty chain and sooty cushion rocks in the breeze. The grass has been trimmed short, but has gone yellow in need of water. A green garden hose coils like a snake in a pile of leaves next to an old rake by the gate.

"Should we knock?"

"Let's look around."

Lilli totters on her heels across the lawn to the side gate.

She whistles. TOOOT.

"They don't seem to have a dog, let's go."

Angora looks nervous. She follows Lilli with her senses tense and tuned. The two women edge along the side of the house past three trash cans. Lilli lifts the lid. The garbage is bagged up tight. A host of flies shoot up at her face.

"What's that music?"

"Sounds like an old crooner, Russ Colombo maybe."

"Weird."

Lilli has her back flush to the outside wall of the house. Angora keeps her arms folded into her chest.

"You gotta see this."

A young man stands naked, hands braced on his knees, with his face obscured by the angle. His head is shaved. An older man pumps his ass from behind, a long, curved cock slides in and out of a lubricated sphincter.

"Is that Mort?"

The old man, like a well-greased fuck machine, pumps rough and rhythmic with sedulous focus. The silver hair on his back glistens with sweat. His cock slips in and out of the young ass. The mechanical intercourse gets more intense as the man wants to cum. A wad of semen shoots onto the young man's lower back, which the older guy rubs into the skin like a balm. A tenderness falls over the scene as the couple embrace and kiss on the lips and drink each other like cool water. The younger man nestles his ear in a forest of argent-colored chest hair, the older man envelops his lover in strong arms and strokes his shaved head.

"Is it Mort?"

•••

Mort's blue eyes are gone.

Negdin looks more like a pile of viscera than a man as he deflates inside his rotten silk drawers like a piece of fruit fallen from a tree.

The flies! The flies!

## NINETEEN

Cubby hangs upside down from the monkey bars. The back of his knees curve around the slick metal. His arms extend toward the ground and his shirt hangs over the lower part of his face which is flushed. He imagines himself to be a bat in its cave. He's held this position since the start of recess, his previous record—five minutes—has already been shattered.

Yadira sits in the sandbox. One leg tucked under, chin rested on the knobby knee of the other leg. She digs a hole in pursuit of a black and yellow sand bee and holds one of her shoes like a hammer to pound the creature when it pops up.

The playground's rife with activity. A fugue of shrill voices—shouts, squawks, laughter—floats over the blacktop like a sonic haze. The dismal sky still looks like dry gray cement. A gull circles over the lunch arbor. Broderick Penny kicks a lopsided ball against a wall.

"Four hundred and one, four hundred and two."

His brother Cleo argues with a kid from another class in a four-square match.

"Liners are takeovers. Everyone knows that chump."

"You're out."

"No, you're out!"

The two boys step up face to face. Little chest to little chest. Third grade button noses clash when brown eyes meet. As tough as kittens are feisty. On the other side of the playground two boys run toward the water fountain like kamikazes. The Yard Duty, Mrs. Pyre, aka "Cragface," blows her whistle and shakes her crooked finger. "Now get over here and walk, don't run…"

"Come on then."

"No, you come on!"

"Take it over."

"Yeah, come on."

"Hurry! The bell's gonna ring."

Cleo steps back into the serve position and hits the ball into one of the other squares. Igor returns it. Cleo slaps the ball to his adversary, but the boy sends it back with a tricky spin. Cleo answers the challenge and smacks it toward the boy's face. The boy from the other class swings wildly and knocks the ball out of bounds where a girl at the hopscotch court kicks it across the playground.

"Chase it!".

"You chase it!"

Yadira tracks the sand bee like a radar. She lowers her foot and extinguishes it like a cigarette.

"What you doing girl?"

"None of your business."

This is their first confrontation since Yadira borrowed Brenda's purple crayon without permission in second grade.

Braids had been yanked.

"You're a murderer like your daddy. Your daddy's a cop killer. Ooo. They say he gonna get the gas chamber. The man on the tv say your daddy gonna die. And you too. You bee killer. You bee killer. You like your daddy, the way you stomp that bee, the way he shoot that cop. Oooo. You daddy gonna burn in hell. That's what they say in church. The minister say your daddy a bad man. Ooo. You all gonna burn."

"You're a liar!"

A group of children swarm to the fight like bees around a dropped soda can.

"Your daddy is a killer. He shot a police man in the back. Your daddy's a killer and my daddy says he's a coward for shooting that officer in the back. The minister in my church say God is gonna punish your daddy fo' ever."

"My dad didn't shoot anybody! You're jealous because the thrift store gives your family clothes and your mama smells like a pack of skunks!"

Cubby looks at the world upside down. His head feels heavier. Why is Yadira shouting down from the bleached-out sky? The children gathered around the fight are like stalactites accreted along the roof of a cave. He's a vampire bat now, wait 'til nighttime.

The kids stand like megalithic monuments circled about the druidic ritual sacrifice. Cubby observes the action between shoulders. His head throbs like a black sun on the winter solstice.

"Ooo, you gonna let her say yo' mama stinky?"

"Heh girl, don't let her bad mouth your daddy."

"Mind your own beeswax."

Brenda stands a head taller than Yadira. Her uniform seems a degree shabbier since she inherited it from her sister who moved on to middle school. Brenda's mother works in a fish market and comes home covered with impure slime and guts—the intense smell makes Brenda want to puke. She feels embarrassed.

"Your mother stinks like fish and your father has Prader-Willis."

"Don't drag my family into your shame!"

She follows her retort with a straight jab to Yadira's metallic-green eye. The blood vessel POP makes the spectators' nerves shiver like nails on a chalkboard. The circle tightens. Goose pimples swell on the mob's upper arms. Cubby can no longer see through the gaps between the bodies.

"Ooo, you gonna let her hit you like that?"

At this point the blood in Cubby's head congeals. He loses consciousness and drops from the bars like a sack of potatoes. His face meets the ground and the rough sand is driven into his cheeks by the hammer force of the boy's trunk and limbs barreling down.

The THUMP is so loud that the combatants release grip on each other's hair, the circle cracks like an egg and reforms around Cubby's limp body heaped below the monkey bars.

The mob moves like an amoeba from event to event. Yadira leaves the fight behind and pushes in to help her friend.

Some of the kids think maybe he's dead.

"Cubby, can you hear me?"

As Cubby regains consciousness, his teacher's face appears, large and somewhat blurry.

"Owww."

"Are you alright Zazuzay?"

"No."

Cubby turns his neck to the left. He recognizes the nurse's office. The cot where he'd lain with a stomach ache feels cold. He looks around at the clock that ticks backwards, the containers of bandages and the jar of antiseptic that stings scraped knees.

"E-J-S-P-L."

The teacher stands up and flicks a speck of dust off the eye chart.

"Always a smart aleck, eh Mr. Zazuzay?" To the nurse he says, "I have to get back to class. The school sub can't handle that bunch. I left him showing *Say Goodbye*. 'And thus, we enforce our dominion over the creatures of the earth.'"

Cubby shifts his gaze to the nurse, tries to focus on her white coat. She smells like cigarette smoke.

"He'll be alright. I called his mother, but she's not home."

"Typical. Maybe that fall will knock some sense into him."

Cubby catches sight of the bruise that swells up under one of his blue eyes in the mirror. The abrasions left by the gravel remind him of his dad's three-day stubble. Everyone says he has his father's nose and now with the gapped tooth and this new black eye, he sees his dad in the mirror. As he pats at his hair for a bald spot, he imagines his belly expanding by quarter inches year on year around the middle. In a confused voice he says, "Dad."

## TWENTY

The judge raps the gavel against the sound block—the sharp report rings familiar in Jimenez's ear. He's heard this sound, or one like it, muffled between states of consciousness. He remembers leaning against the window of his '69 Impala; Yadira was asleep in the seat belt.

The INS agent had taken Silvia away in a black Chevy Caprice with tinted windows.

"You pigs got better things to do, eh?"

Yaz feels the steel cuff close on his wrist, squeeze tighter, so it chokes the circulation to his right hand. There are at least two other people in the alley, possible witnesses, a blonde, looking to turn a trick or score dope. The other is a crack addict and known stool pigeon, who'd sell his children for a toke. He senses the baton before it crashes into the back of his head.

He lives in that instant before the blackout. After that, darkness closed over him like a tomb.

The judge's austere eyes scan her notes. She wears the stern countenance the job requires like a mask. Some of the men on death row, based on little more than anecdotal evidence, call her "The Queen of Hearts." In fact, the number of men she has written warrants on, to die by gas under California's death penalty, rivals but does not exceed any sitting judge.

Jimenez and his lawyer wear suits—Jimenez insisted on his best black drape with long tails, a vintage tie pinned with a gold tack. He looks a bit like the young Cab Calloway. Cecil had to demand his client be allowed to shave.

His hair is waxed with Royal Crown into a sick pompadour. His brown and white spectator wingtips feel rich on his feet. Cecil bought him a new pair of dress socks. Jimenez swells with confidence inspired by innocence. He is anxious to say, "Not guilty." His hands are cuffed behind his back and the leg irons feel heavy around his ankles.

The court clerk reads the charge. Her mask is harder to interpret—her clothes, features and manner are unremarkable. It's hard to see her as a person forging a home life, burdened with thoughts, aches and yearnings.

"Mr. Yaz."

"Present."

"The state of California charges Jimenez Yaz, a human being, with capital murder in the first degree of David Jones, a human being. The state also ascribes special circumstances, since the victim was a police officer killed in the line of duty. The alleged incident took place on November 25th of this year…"

Jimenez looks around the court facility. He'd written a thousand words of unimpeachable copy about how the city bilked the taxpayers in its construction. He compared the hardwood panels to gold candlesticks in the Pope's boudoir. There are a million men in US prisons, thousands who have died in lock up across California and 514 souls languishing on death row.

"Do you understand the charge?"

He looks into her cold eyes.

"I understand."

"How do you plead?"

"I can only plead not guilty your honor, since I never shot anybody."

"Counselor, do you have a bail recommendation?"

"Yes, your honor. My client has been brutalized by the police since his incarceration. I have a statement from a doctor that his injuries occurred after he was taken into custody. We ask that he's released on a bond of no more than ten thousand dollars."

"The state objects, your honor. This guy killed a police officer. We recommend he be held without bail. Add to that his previous arrest record and his association with militant Chicano terrorists."

The judge scans a sheet of paper handed to her by the clerk.

"Based on the preliminary evidence the court remands you to custody without bail. Be advised that you have the right to a speedy trial by jury of your peers…"

Jimenez pictures his peers decked out in their Sunday suits as they fill the jury box—a line of tricked out Impalas and '47 Caddy lowriders cruise the parking lot. He pictures Mort, with his strong sense of provocation as an artist, ordered to leave the courtroom after he arrives in a judge's robe or a copper's uniform.

"We'd like to request a change of venue due to pre-trial publicity."

"Denied, Mr. Gonococci. This city is big enough to handle dozens of high-profile cases each year. I see no reason why we can't handle this one."

"Have you ever tried a homicide?" Jimenez asks.

"No, not yet," his lawyer replies.

The judge raps her gavel one last time for dramatic emphasis.

## TWENTY-ONE

The hearse slows at the intersection near Taylor Way. Lilli turns the wheel and the power steering delivers the Caddy onto a tree-lined street haunted by conspicuous absence of human life. The lawns in this neighborhood seem greener than the ones near Mt. Hope. A "For Sale" sign has been posted in front of a house tented for termites, it looks like they cut down an old tree in the front yard, so potential buyers can get a better view. Just a stump remains.

The Cadillac hearse rolls down the block and the engine purrs like a feral cat. A boy peeks from behind the blinds in one of the houses. As Lilli scans for the address, some of the houses have the number painted on the curb while others have wooden block letters on the garage door. A few numbers appear on mailboxes.

"...so the last time I went to the airport the metal detector went off. The guard had me take off a bracelet. But it went off again. So, he got the hand-held detector. The wand made a little beep as it passed over my right tit. The guard looked embarrassed, poor guy—he was an older gentleman, you know. Back over my tit and it beeped again. Over the left tit. It beeped. I smiled and shrugged. He waved the wand over my pussy and the detector went crazy! BEEP BEEP BEEP!"

"1332 Taylor!"

"He musta thought I had a gun shoved up my twat…"

The hearse slows to a stop in front of Negdin's house.

"It looks haunted."

Lilli surveys the weeds, a few daisies push out of the loam in what must have been the garden. There's a broken slat on the sooty fence and wild vines growing around the house front. The interior beyond the window is occluded by thickly drawn drapes.

"Looks like a crack den."

"It would be like Mort to hide out, stoned out of his mind. In search of Bohemia…There's our car."

"Kicking the gong around."

Lilli locks The Club to the steering wheel. She hits the kill switch behind the seat, steps out onto the street, locks and shuts the door. She presses the alarm BEEP BOOP.

A melody of ice cream truck music filters down through the trees from an adjacent street. The beat-up Toyota sits in the driveway, with the driver's side window rolled down. A scruffy gray cat leaps out of the window.

"Did you see that cat? His eyes were different colors."

"Smells like it peed."

Angora opens the door, touches the seat.

As she climbs in, the wire frame of the seat presses against the small of her back. The Club is locked in place on their car too; the Del Shannon 8-track still hangs from the mouth of the player.

Angora reaches into the glove compartment and picks up a plastic bag of brown incense sticks. She presses one to her nostrils.

Lilli produces a Zippo from her purse. The butane flame touches the incense stick and a plume of smoke dribbles out. Angora lodges it in the ashtray.

"Mmm, raspberry."

"Now what?"

"Let's ring the doorbell."

The play seems too simple, but after what they saw in Mt. Hope, it makes sense.

Angora takes the lead up the walk toward the front door. Lilli follows close behind. As she teeters on her tango heels, the leaves crinkle underfoot.

"This place needs work."

"Maybe we should call the police. What if the old man's a serial killer."

"That would be fantastic… I've spoken with a lot of serial killers though, you know, when we visited them in prison. They have a vibe."

"Most people don't ask strangers to write suicide notes. Don't you think it's morbid to capitalize off depression like that? Mort is so…"

"He wanted to make money for you and Cubby. He said to buy a house."

"I've never heard him say he wanted to own a house. He always says, 'a house owns you' and that he would have to work all the time and pull weeds on weekends. He'd rather spend time on his art than save up money for a new roof. Maybe he's right, houses are like $100,000 now. Too much."

"Well yeah, we talked a lot at the museum."

"He refuses to talk about serious issues at home. I try and try but he changes the subject or tunes out. We get in arguments because he won't get in an argument.

BING BONG.

They strain to hear the slightest footfall inside the house. Angora lets out the breath they held; Lilli presses her ear to the door.

"I don't hear anything."

"Try the knocker."

Lilli lifts it and bangs five times.

They wait. Not a sound. Even the ice cream truck music has faded out.

"How do you communicate with PT?"

"Well one time PT wanted to have sex at this party. And I wasn't into it. He really wanted to. He gets so randy. Like a satyr you know. A real horndog. That was the first real test when I told him 'No.' He explained how horny he was and I explained why I wasn't into it and we came to a consensus to fuck two times when we got home."

Half way through her story she remembered that she'd jerked him off in the bathroom at the party, but decided to leave that part out.

"Now what?"

Lilli reaches down and pushes the door; it opens.

In moments before you pass through a door like this, you have to expect that what lies on the other side will change your entire life. Angora pushes the door which creaks ajar and offers the first glimpse of the menagerie. She recalls over-stuffed cartoon closets—Tennessee Tuxedo and his trusty sidekick Chumley. Lilli thinks of flea markets, antique stores, junk yards. PT would love that elk for the museum. She had an aunt, another lover of old things, who hoarded. She couldn't bear to throw "perfectly good stuff" away. Angora admires a cedar armoire in the corner and feels confused by the box of a thousand spoons. She almost trips over a bucket set in the middle of the floor to catch a drip the last time it rained. When was the last time it rained? Lilli walks past the mannequin head and thumbs through a stack of canvases.

"These paintings are good."

"Hello! Mort are you in here?"

A faint electrical hum beckons the women from the hall.

"Do you hear that?"

"Sounds like my vibrator."

A single strand of cobweb catches Lilli's red hair. She wriggles out of the web and casts it to the floor.

"Look at this stuff."

Her eyes shift across rugs, lamps, chairs, boxes and more paintings. The severed head of the mannequin looks up at them.

"This place is creepy."

"I don't think anybody's here."

She kicks the box of a thousand spoons, which jangles loud enough to alert the dead.

"I feel like someone's watching."

Lilli's foot falls on a creaky floorboard and the sound travels to Angora's stomach.

"What's that smell?"

Lilli recognizes it. Some artifacts that find their way into the museum are steeped in this mal odor, which most humans find repulsive, though spend enough time and a subtle aphrodisiac essence, like dead flowers kept after the wedding, will cut through the fouled air. A smell like making love in the county morgue. Hemingway called it the "Smell of Death."

"The sound shifted. It's more buzz than hum now."

"I say we call the police."

Angora's fear seeks authority over her muscular coordination. Her gait slows near point zero. The unknown force that pulsates from the center of the house feels like the antithesis of life, a bane to breath.

"Some of my friends are cops, but..."

Lilli makes the first step into the hallway.

Angora's grip closes around Lilli's stalwart arm.

"Oh Hon', breaking into strange houses makes me feel weird too. I've read so many accounts of the Manson family, but never creepy-crawled someone's home…"

Tired of being the ticket agent in the theater booth, she wants to be the action hero, the stunt driver. Not some casual observer. She wants to gather suspects in a room and wow them with a spellbinding delineation of her brilliant deduction. She understands why detectives need a sidekick or wisecracking moll to bounce ideas off. Solving mysteries alone would feel, well… lonely. Like voyeurism or masturbation.

Angora doesn't want to be a hero or anybody's sidekick. She wants to go home. As the buzz intensifies, it sounds less real. It's in my head. It's like a string vibrating. It's intuition. Why would a sound want to kill me? Her sanity takes a punch to the jaw. The sound wants to sweep her children into the vortex. She's in a death trap, on a death trip. Spinning out of control. BUZZ! What the fuck is that sound? Her grip tightens on Lilli's arm. BUZZ!

"Cubby!"

"Angora! Calm down sweetie. It's me Lilli. Cubby's safe at school."

"Aaagghh!" Angora screams. "I huh… I huh to se… I, huh… Mort!"

Angora's voice caves in like a parking garage in an earthquake. It tumbles down around her as concrete rubble and asbestos dust bury her in an avalanche of fear. She wants to cry. Feels broken.

"I saw Mort floating in the hall."

Lilli believes in ghosts, wants to see. Yearns. But there's nothing there. They stumble in somnambulance toward the green door, agape like a mouth, everything you know is wrong. Life's a ruse and your faith in reality is bogus. Mort was right. It's all a sham.

The smell is pure sulfur. Angora flings herself through the green door and jogs down the stairs into the room. Lilli follows. Ten thousand flies swarm the thick air. On the other side of the humid cloud, the diabolical suicide machine reveals itself in its unhinged horror.

Lilli is astounded. The knife-wielding-tentacles of the machine wrap themselves around a limp body in a rude wooden chair. A pair of skeleton arms free of the flesh that held them in the wrist restraints splay outward. Another body, a shape without form, is spread across the floor.

The contents of their stomachs fling themselves into the scene to witness the horror first hand.

"Ooo-ahhh No! No! Mort!"

She runs into the cloud of flies. Her stomach wants to throw itself up through her esophagus.

"Mort."

Lilli loses sight of her as ten thousand tiny black insects scatter. She stands awe-struck in the doorway.

Death is omnipresent.

"You fucker!"

She pounds her fists on Mort's rotten corpse. One solid punch to the intact part of his skull, garroted by a thin iron collar—POPS—and THUMPS on the floor next to Negdin's maggot jelly boxer shorts.

"You stupid fucker! You have a son! You have a son and a daughter who need you! You have a daughter."

She drops to her knees and grabs Mort's festered leg.

"You have a wife who needs you."

The dismembered leg pulls free of his hip joint and she takes it in a fall to the floor. She hugs the limb like a stuffed animal in the moment before sleep.

"I need you."

Lilli summons courage and purses her lips tight. She ducks into the insolent storm of flies—weaned on human flesh, they crawl on her mouth, ears, eyes. The wings and legs and bodies caress in a way she's never been touched.

Lilli reaches blind for Angora. Her shirt snags on one of the knives. The insects are all over her. A sharp poke intervenes… as the syringe in the grip of the machine jabs into the fleshy part of her ass.

"Rrrrr."

Lilli's strong hand hooks Angora's shirt and drags her through the carrion; she slides over maggots in the offal and slips through feculent vomit to safety at the base of the stairs.

## TWENTY-TWO

1970. Mort, age four, sits on his youngest uncle's lap under the Xmas tree. His teeth glimmer, large, perfect, white. He holds a football bigger than his head. It's too big to get a grip on. The tree is decorated with ruddy matte colors, brick red bulbs and silver tinsel. Mort wears a fake Indian costume, moccasins and a vinyl headband with a cadmium yellow feather.

His hippie aunt sits pretzel-legged next to him. Her long straight dirty-blonde hair frames a troubled face, burdened with quiet disquiet. A friend, also glum-faced, sits on the floor next to her. He half-smiles dumbly in a brown leather coat. His dark brown hair hangs past his shoulders.

Somebody got a new Hi-Fi system—the wood grain matches the coffee and end tables. It goes well with the sofa. Waxy bubbles rodilate inside an orange lava lamp.

His oldest uncle shows off his new sedan. It has a big flower painted on the side. He wears Buddy Holly glasses and a Greek fisherman's cap. Mort's dad has a goatee, short hair and wears a black turtleneck.

Mort's mother chases her middle brother into the kitchen with a towel rolled into a rat's tail. The brother cowers, with his hands up to deflect the whip. The wet corner of the towel cracks near his ear. He holds a cigarette between two fingers, hair down to the middle of his back.

One of the hippies put an early Pink Floyd album on the Hi-Fi.

Gran says, "Turn it down."

Mort's Gran sits on the sofa with her husband. She holds a Lucky Strike in her left hand. Her lungs are already tar papered black. The husband seems older, bald, with thick corrective eye glasses. He wears dress slacks and a proper shirt with one of those pocket protectors.

He remembers quieter Xmases, a model train set that ran round the tree.

Stairs twist like a colon into the basement bowels of the house. He's got a lathe, a drill press, a band saw, three grinders… The machines seem like they were designed for singular, sinister tasks. Most of the machines in the shop stand taller than Mort and all have been painted battleship gray.

"You can look, but don't touch."

The tools are like alien technology from a science fiction movie. They have teeth and lights that flicker and make inhuman WHIRRS, HUMS and BUZZES.

A year passes with the turn of a page. Cubby examines Xmas 1971. Somebody got a new queen-sized bed. The Polaroid looks darker than it should. The drapes should have been pulled wide; there's not enough light.

His father looks happy. Little Morty's arms are raised in elation after he hits a strike with a plastic bowling ball. He wears brown corduroys and a striped shirt.

Cubby's grandpa unwraps a new clock, set in the hull of a model tall ship. His goatee has been shaved. He wears a beaded necklace and open shirt.

The hippies look dead tired. Mort's youngest uncle has bags under his eyes. The blonde aunt still looks despondent. Family gatherings aren't her thing. One of her boyfriends must have announced that posed pictures taken on holidays were "square" or "bourgeois." In the photo, he has long hair, denim jeans, a suede fringe jacket. He puts a flute into its case.

Mort's Gran sits alone in a green chair and smokes Lucky Strikes. She wonders if she'll have any more grandchildren. Somebody took a picture of the food laid out. A basket of dinner rolls, a dish of white mints.

"Hey Gran, where's grandpa Linden?"

"He's no longer with us."

Her voice is sweet, it comforts, resonant with melancholia, a brush against sorrow for the first time. She exhales a cloud of smoke.

"He was shot," she says after a moment.

"Like in a cowboy movie?"

"Yes, Honey, but don't worry."

She takes a drag from her cigarette. Linden waves the gun that he keeps locked in the basement.

"I will not tolerate marijuana in this house."

His threat to shoot the blonde hippie aunt became more serious when he fired a shot into the wall. She could see in her husband's dilated eyes that he wasn't himself. He'd never sat with a bottle of bourbon at the kitchenette late into the night before they forced him to retire.

She knew how lonely he felt. The cop at the door tried to convince him to put the gun down. She replays in slow motion the moment her husband turned the pistol on himself. She remembers the dope smell in her daughter's hair. The barrel pressed up against his temple. The strain showed in his malignant eyes. He wasn't himself. The second shot delivered his brains over the wall. The cop dropped his head with regret. One of her sons was there to clean up, he got on his knees to scrub the blood off the porch.

"Who shot him, Gran?"

The idea of suicide seems so alien, so inhuman. She takes another drag on her Lucky Strike. The smoke fills her lungs.

"A bad man, he was shot by a bad man."

She doesn't cry. Mort runs a finger across her brow—her wrinkles remind him of the growth rings in an old tree—fire, famine, flood—every lightning strike and pestilent year, every wet spring and every dry summer there to read for anyone who cares to look.

Mort lies awake, the dark shadows outside his window seem to move. Are those footsteps? The sound filters through the pillow pulled around his ears. A fantasia of color scintillates through his imagination—the shadows phase through oxblood and hunter green. The shadows have hue like sounds have texture. Falling toward sleep, the aliens come for him. A big-headed scaly green human-oid disintegrates his father with a ray gun. His mother stands undaunted before the creature. She won't back down. Mort stands behind her, uneasy at best.

## TWENTY-THREE

Angora sits in front of a computer screen in the back room at the Death Museum. Mort's notebook sets awkwardly propped open with a coffee mug full of red wine, which leaves a vermillion ring. The wine bottle, half full, sits to the right of the monitor. Joy Division's *She's Lost Control* plays low in the background on the stereo as she pecks with two fingers at the keys and copies from his text—her nails have been painted with a color called "Smog."

"Oh, Mort, this is so hard."

She takes a sip of wine. Her hair remains in the precise bob. Writing good, strong sentences takes labor. She'd like to put the text in her own words, but which words? She has wrestled with it for hours and, slowly, watched the prose soften and become more personal, shy of elegiac— her voice painted with grief adds a feminine angle to this disconsolate "chants des morts."

Cubby plays with his action figures on a long green couch at the far side of the room; Yadira reads a book on one end while the pig snores at the other.

"Hey Lilli, could you change the music?"

"Oh sure, I was just trying to set the proper tone."

"Mort used to listen to this album when he felt depressed. He said it was so full of sorrow, it could get under his mood and lift him up."

"Hi, Aunt Lilli."

"Hi Cub. Hey Yoyo."

"Mmm."

Lilli has cut her hair shorter though it's still bright red. She wears the same tango heels and a baby-doll style tee, with the word *Hole* printed in pink letters. A moment of silence in the room is broken by John Doe and Exene Cervenka, of the Los Angeles punk band X, singing *The Unheard Music*. With Billy Zoom on guitar.

"How's the letter?"

"Pretty good, since I've never used a computer. Can you show me the spell checker?"

"Oh sure, it's easy. Mrs. Castel will be here at three."

Angora looks around for a clock.

"I swapped out Mr. Negdin's personal details for the one's Mrs. Castel gave me and started making changes. She gave me this 'last words' quote, but I think we should cut it."

"It's alright, we can print two versions."

"I've gone over some of these lines ten times. It'll never be finished—so I better fix the spelling and let it go."

"I asked her to bring a cashier's check. In the notebook, Mort was dead-set against personal checks, since some people do it for financial pressures."

"A ten-thousand-dollar money order, yowzah."

"We'll have enough to cover the rent and start up our freak animal farm."

"To the Freak Farm."

Gemini, the two-butted chicken, promenades across the room and pecks hither and thither for edible bits.

"Gabba gabba…"

"One of us. One of us!"

"Kill em and eat em," PT adds and raises a Heineken.

"PT, you startled me. I didn't know you were here."

Lilli raises her glass to the Grecian urn which holds Mort's ashes in the corner and says, "To our old friend!"

Angora turns back to the note, unable to raise a cup for her husband. His death is still too painful or her widowhood too hectic. She realizes that grief and mourning are not the same thing. You can go through the rituals, go to the funeral and close the casket, you can wear black and be done with wearing black, but grief has its own timeline. Mort would've never gotten over my death, she thinks. She misses his stupid exhortations, "Be strong Angora," "Be stoic," "Be brave." Oh, Mort, I wish you were here with me now.

Cubby tries to recall a detail about his father. He thinks of the Mouse Trap and smiles.

"Well, to Mr. Negdin for leaving you that house in the suburbs."

Angora looks over at Cubby and Yadira on the couch and smiles.

"I like our new house Mom."

"I like it too, Honey, now that we got it cleaned up. The estate sale was murder. But, now, I have to get this work done."

"I gotta finish setting up the new exhibit. Lilli, you wanna help me install the syringe arm?"

Lilli rubs the blackened sore spot where she took the jab and shows PT her middle finger.

"Click on this icon."

She puts her hand on top of Angora's and guides the mouse through the operation. It takes time to correct the spelling, but they get it done.

"It looks good."

"Print it."

"Put that thick fancy paper in the printer."

"Should we print more copies of the questionnaire?"

"We can do that later."

A few seconds later, the completed suicide note clatters out of the printer. Lilli carries the finished note up to the front of the museum to wait for Mrs. Castel.

Angora squeezes close to her daughter on the couch and pushes Yadira's hair out of her green eyes. Their nails match. It's a hot spring day and the little girl sweats under her heavy 80%-dark-chocolate-bar locks. Bedlam takes up more than his share of the couch. The two-butted chicken struts around the room like it owns the place.

"I was trying to teach Cubby to whistle, but he won't listen."

"Don't give up, he'll get it."

"Hey Mom, does that Chet guy have to come for dinner?"

"Mr. King's a nice man."

"He looks like Bedlam." Bedlam grunts and shivers in his sleep; he appears to be dreaming.

"Cubby, be respectful to Mr. King."

"Mom, how did dad die?"

Angora had found an old notebook in Mort's desk where he requested that his body be donated to science, but the scientists said there wasn't much they could use.

After the autopsy, the coroner couldn't pin down the exact cause of death. He'd been poisoned, stabbed, shot, strangled and electrocuted. The coroner stated that brain death occurred around 6:00pm, but the post-mortem exam couldn't rule out any of the means, such was the precision of Mr. Negdin's machine. He couldn't even say if Mort strapped himself in willingly. So, "Death by Misadventure" was listed as the final verdict.

Cremation was the best option. He had always said he didn't want a funeral—though one contradictory entry in his notebook implied burial, "A memorial headstone would be nice, a place for people to sit on the grass and think about my body of work…"

"Body of work," Ha! Show me the body!

The local newspaper made a big deal out of Mort's death. The crazy suicide machine made good copy, so she wouldn't be able to shelter Cubby from it forever. Even if it was an accident, Cubby would one day have to ask himself why his dad went down in the basement.

# SATANIC DEATH MACHINE!

## SUICIDE FOR ARTIST FRIEND OF COP KILLER

The art collectors beat on the door at ridiculous hours. Angora considered selling off Negdin's paintings, but sent most away empty-handed. She looked through Mort's papers and the sketches. She sold an unfinished sculpture to a man from New York for a thousand dollars and later realized Cubby put it together in second grade.

She sold a pair of Mort's underwear to a collector from some small museum in Texas. She shouldn't have burned his tampon, snot and ear wax painting. That health hazard would be worth a fortune.

Cubby asked to keep The Perpetual Stasis Machine, which he moved to the top of his own dresser drawers.

"It's hard for me to explain, Honey."

She sees her husband's Norwegian blue eyes… runs a finger over Mort's eyebrows on her son's face.

"He got shot."

"Who shot him mama?"

She clicks the "Shut Down" button on the monitor. The screen makes a sound like electricity getting smaller.

"A bad man."

"I miss him mama."

"Me too, Cubby. Me too.

Angora gathers her children in her arms and hugs them to her bosom. She takes the last sip from the mug of wine and the notebook springs shut.

She feels like crying and lets a tear fall.

# CODA

This is it. People wonder about Van Gogh. Did he do it? Whatever his end, it has nothing to do with his painting. Nothing to do with color, light, shape. Okay, there's madness in it, in the work, but really I've found more beauty in painting than in a sunset. People say I followed Rothko everywhere. No, I chased the same feeling he did. He caught it, many times, on canvas, and I didn't. That's the difference. In some ways I inherited this end from my father. I'm glad I lived to hear someone call him a genius. My mother never thought so. It's funny to think of them, gone so long, at this hour. All my life I worried about what I'd leave behind. I tried to make things that would survive me. Well, if I learned anything in this late hour, it is the nonsense of this idea. This is my decision. My way to retain some dignity. When other people hate you, it's not important. When your body hates you, you have to listen. Thank you.

I don't blame anyone for it, it wasn't your fault.

Leif Negdin

DMSD
548 5<sup>th</sup> Avenue
SD, CA 92101
1 (888)-SUI-CIDE

Well, that's the end of the vodka.



In old books bad women always try ⟨...⟩ was thought better, I guess, than being whatever it was they didn t want you to be. I always wished the author would find some clever way out. But now I understand. It's hard, this life. I did my best. I tried and now I'm tired. I want a rest. I leave everything to my daughters. I wish I could leave more. I don't want to be a burden. I've done everything I came to do. And more. So much more than so many people. I've loved, I've hated. I've been madly jealous and stirred mad jealousy (my daughters don't know this about me, but I loved. I really loved.) In a few months or a year, I would be gone anyway. So, my lovelies. This is it. June is such a soft month for a nap.

Mrs. Barbara Castel

DMSD
548 5th Avenue
SD, CA 92101
1 (888)-SUI-CIDE

In old books bad women always try suicide. It was thought better, I guess, than being whatever it was they didn't want you to be. I always wished the author would find some clever way out. But now I understand. It's hard, this life. I did my best. I tried and now I'm tired. I want a rest. I leave everything to my daughters. I wish I could leave more. I don't want to be a burden. I've done everything I came to do. And more. So much more than so many people. I've loved, I've hated. I've been madly jealous and stirred mad jealousy (my daughters don't know this about me, but I loved. I really loved.) In a few months or a year, I would be gone anyway. So, my lovelies. This is it. June is such a soft month for a nap.

Mrs. Barbara Castel

# SOUNDTRACK FOR A DEATH MUSEUM

## Side A

Circle Jerks - Live Fast, Die Young

Dead Kennedys - Police Truck

Cadillac Tramps - Cadillac Hearse

Dead Boys - Sonic Reducer

Thought Criminals - More Suicides Please

Suicide - Ghost Rider

D.I. – Richard Hung Himself

MDC - Dead Cops

999 - Homicide

Jim Carroll Band - It's Too Late

Misfits - Last Caress

## Side B

Bad Religion - Drastic Actions

Stooges - Death Trip

Siouxsie and the Banshees - Helter Skelter

The Dwarves - I Wish That I Was Dead

Gravedigger V – Spooky

Joy Division - Atrocity Exhibition

Bauhaus - Rosegarden Funeral of Sores

Daniel Johnston - Funeral Home

## Bonus Tracks

The Cramps - Human Fly

TSOL - Code Blue

The Bags - We Will Bury You

Suicidal Tendencies - Suicidal Failure

SNFU - Cannibal Café

Allen Ginsberg - Father Death Blues

*Photo by Anthony Scoggins*

I have written poetry, short fiction, long fiction & non-fiction. My history of DIY publishing extends to the early 90s, though my novel *The Sub* was published by Incommunicado Press in 1996. I was also honored to be the featured writer for City Works in 2002. I spent six years writing *The Book of Books* which Rich Ferguson called my "magnum opus."

I was born in 1966. I lived with my daughter's mom for 30 years before we got married on our 30th anniversary. I choose day jobs that leave me energy for writing, the best was The Museum of Death. I love books and have a home library with 3,423 volumes. I collect books from small presses like AK, Exact Change, Manic D, Black Sparrow, New Directions, City Lights & Re/Search.

I'm a veteran spoken word artist, fortunate to have shared a stage with many of my favorite writers:

Steve Abee, Linda Albertano, Dave Alvin, Don Bajema, Liz Belile, Iris Berry, Angela Boyce, Derrick Brown, Dennis Cooper, Creedle, Kimberly Dark, Sharon Elise, Maggie Estep, Raymond Federman, Rich Ferguson, Larry Fondation, reg e gaines, Weba Garretson, Pleasant Gehman, Gary Glazner, Daphne Gottlieb, Barry Graham, Cecil Hayduke, Stevie Harris, Michael Hemmingson, Stewart Home, Hank Hyena, Tamara Johnson, Shawna Kenney, Michael Klam, The Last Poets, Mary Leary, Beth Lisick, Lob, Jon Longhi, Richard Loranger, Lydia Lunch, Douglas A. Martin, Ellyn Maybe, Larry McCaffery, Jeffrey McDaniel, June Melby, Joe Milosch, minerva, Mindy Nettifee, Matthew Niblock, Alexis O'Hara, Nicole Panter, Peter Plate, Clebo Rainey, El Rivera, La Ruocco, Michelle Serros, Several Girls Galore, Shappy, Bucky Sinister, Hal Sirowitz, The Taco Shop Poets, Jervey Tervalon, Juliette Torrez, Tarin Towers, Quincy Troupe, Chris Vannoy, Lizzie Wann, Pam Ward, Ted Washington, Saul Williams, William Upski Wimsatt & The Watts Prophets. I have performed at The SDSU Avant-garde Festival, The Fringe Fest, SXSW, The National Poetry Slam & Lollapalooza 94.

www.ingramcontent.com/pod-product-compliance
Lightning Source LLC
Chambersburg PA
CBHW070342200726
48294CB00003B/755